HOW TO KEEP A WEREWOLF

AND OTHER EXOTIC PETS WHICH MAY OR MAY NOT
A) EXIST
OR
B) EAT YOU

Fiona Bowron
Illustrations by Tom Jennings

PORTICO

CONTENTS

THERE ARE TWO KINDS OF PEOPLE IN THIS WORLD: THOSE WHO HAVE PETS, AND THOSE WHO HAVE BEIGE CARPET.

Regardless of which category you currently fall into, the fact that you have bothered to pick up this book at all suggests that you already know there is something missing from your life – perhaps something with a wet nose and a furry tummy.

Owning a pet can enrich your life, and bring all sorts of extra dimensions to it that you probably hadn't even considered. And that's quite apart from the moulting.

It has been scientifically proven (by real scientists who probably ought to be working on something more serious) that owning a pet brings many benefits, and since they are described as 'benefits' they are definitely worth having.

Probably.

And we're not just talking about the obvious stuff like having someone to talk to on a long winter evening (even if it *is* just the goldfish, who will most likely forget everything you tell it within a matter of seconds), but more serious scientific stuff, too.

For example, it is now a well-known fact that pet owners tend to be healthier and less stressed than non-pet owners (at least if you edit out the times the cat wakes you at 3am because it fancies a snack, or the dog goes ballistic at your garden gnome for no apparent reason).

Those of us who have pets, naturally, have little need for such scientific vindication. We know instinctively that having a pet is just, well, *right*.

As humans we pride ourselves on our individuality, and of course this is reflected in our choice of pet. Some people want, say, a small furry animal that will sit in a cage and cause very little in the way of inconvenience (at least until it figures out how to get *out* of the cage). Others want larger animals like dogs or horses, so that they can enjoy the benefits of exercising in the great outdoors.

Others prefer cats – who are often only too willing to bring the great outdoors (or, more specifically, small, screaming, furred or feathered members of it) directly to you in your living room.

Perhaps you simply want the kudos of owning an exotic animal, but are unsure if your lifestyle can sustain regular trips out hunting buffalo with your pet. And then, of course, there are all the legal complications of having to obtain licences and permissions.

One way to avoid all this annoying paperwork is to choose a pet which, technically, doesn't exist. At least not yet.

This is not quite as crazy as it may sound.

Let us not forget the Komodo dragon – a large monitor lizard that is now so well known that you can barely switch on the Discovery Channel without tripping over a wildlife documentary about it, but that right up to 1912 was considered no more than a myth.

And what of the coelacanth?

'*What indeed?*' you may ask.

This rather odd-looking fish was thought to have died out along with the dinosaurs. Despite scientists believing the coelacanth to have been extinct for millions of years, it was nevertheless rediscovered, alive and swimming, in 1938 (which was described by many in the scientific community as 'jolly inconvenient').

For the rest of us, however, it represents a perfect example of why you can't always believe what they tell you.

There are many things still unknown to science. It should be noted here that just because indigenous peoples have talked of a particular strange animal for decades, lived alongside it, eaten it, or been eaten *by* it, that doesn't mean it's real.

No.

It's only real if scientists have actually got hold of one, dissected it, and had their photos printed in serious and learned scientific journals, while holding up bits of said creature in a serious and learned sort of way.

Up to that point, it remains a myth. A myth which may, nevertheless, carry you off screaming in the dead of night, but still just a myth. This should be of some comfort to your family as your cries ring out through the darkness, and they hastily divide up your possessions before the myth returns for a second helping.

Science is adding newly discovered species to the catalogue all the time, and we're not just talking about the kind of stuff that is only of interest to taxonomy geeks – like insects with an ever-so-slightly different wing arrangement to their cousins.

Look at the Dracula fish, for example, which scientists assure us doesn't *actually* suck blood (mind you, if you happen to come across one of these while out swimming it's probably best not to put this to the test).

And as recently as 2014 they discovered a cartwheeling spider (who *wouldn't* want one of those rushing wildly towards them across the kitchen floor?).

So the point to all this is to get in quickly and choose your unknown-to-science pet before the authorities catch on and start insisting that you need a licence for it.

This is the bit where we introduce the science of cryptozoology.

Of course, serious scientists will probably tell you that cryptozoology (the study of hidden or unknown species) isn't a science at all, but merely a bunch of hokum spouted by the ill-informed and the mad.

At which point we will simply remind them of the coelacanth, and smile smugly.

The main problem with owning a cryptid (the technical term for one of those supposedly mythological animals) is knowing how to look after it. Take a look in your local paper and you won't find many ads offering baby bigfoots free to a good home, and there is little in the way of obedience classes for werewolves.

What, you may ask, does one feed a baby Mongolian death worm? Is the giant squid a good choice of pet if you live in a penthouse flat?

Whatever your own preference, this book will help you discover the best pet for your lifestyle, together with handy hints on how to obtain and care for your chosen animal.

Arranged conveniently in accordance with your attitude towards excitement, adventure and bandages, the book is designed to be 'dipped into' so that you may quickly locate useful information such as how to remove the budgie from the jaws of your new pet sea monster, should the need arise.

Erm…which, of course, it won't, because sea monsters are well-known for their kind and loving nature. Well, most of them are. OK, one or two of them might possibly try to eat you, but only if you provoke them, and frankly if you can't take a joke maybe you should stick to goldfish.

CRYPTIDS FOR THE BEGINNER

DIP YOUR TOES INTO THE WATER...BUT BE
PREPARED TO PULL THEM BACK OUT A BIT
SHARPISH IF YOU SEE TEETH.

BLOBS

BLOBS, OR GLOBSTERS, AS THEY ARE SOMETIMES KNOWN, ARE CURIOUS MARINE CREATURES THAT WASH UP ON VARIOUS BEACHES AROUND THE WORLD.

It has been suggested that the blobs offer proof of the existence of sea serpents. Experts, however, frequently dismiss them as nothing more than the rotting carcasses of sharks, or (if the experts are feeling particularly jolly) whale blubber.

As a result, none of these so-called experts have yet managed to properly categorise globsters, and it is left to the cryptozoologist (that's you and me!) to discern the truth. In fact, anyone with more than a passing acquaintanceship with these fascinating creatures will testify to their depth of character, their mystery and, indeed, their smell.

No one has successfully managed to breed these creatures in captivity, so if you feel this is the animal which best suits your lifestyle, then you will have to wait for the next one to wash up onshore.

They tend to be extremely large, ranging anywhere from 8 to 30 feet in size. There is also considerable variation in shape, as some have limb-like appendages, some have gills, some have hair, some are basically round, some are basically not.

The main advantage to choosing a blob as a pet is that it is an extremely low-maintenance option. It would be ideal for people who work full-time, or indeed who are away from home for weeks at a time. You could leave this one home alone indefinitely and it would come to no harm. They require very little grooming, and a feeding routine is pretty much optional.

Despite this animal being practically *designed* for those people who just don't have time for a pet, there is a very active owners' club based in Salford, England. The club feeds a vibrant show culture, where owners compete annually for the title of Most Odorous Blob, Best of Breed, etc. The Obedience and Blob Agility sections are perhaps the most fiercely contested of all, although on the whole the competition remains good-natured.

As has already been mentioned, the official line regarding blobs is that they are nothing more than the rotting carcasses of ex-marine life. In short, they are dead.

Nothing, in fact, could be further from the truth. Careful study has revealed that the blobs are not dead, but merely dormant. It has been theorised that, perhaps due to environmental factors, the blobs have entered a hibernation phase. The purpose of this hibernation is unclear, but some have suggested that while the blobs apparently sleep, they are, in fact, plotting – simply awaiting the revolution. Only time will tell, but as a precaution, any prospective blob owner is encouraged to view the 1958 Steve McQueen movie of the same name.

EATS	No one really knows. It's probably not a good idea to leave it home alone with your other pets, though.
LIKES	Home makeover programmes. Reality television.
DISLIKES	Steve McQueen movies.

OZARK HOWLER

ONE OF MANY CRYPTIDS IMAGINATIVELY NAMED FOR THE REGION IN WHICH IT HAS BEEN SPOTTED, THE HOWLER HAILS FROM REMOTE AREAS OF THE OZARK MOUNTAINS IN ARKANSAS.

This one is a bit special. The howler is a large, uncatalogued cat, about the size of a bear – so it will require a slightly larger carry basket than your average moggie when you need to take it to the vet. On the plus side, it has a big shaggy coat which makes it absolutely one of the most huggable cryptids you will ever find.

In the wild, the animal is known more for the cries it emits than for its appearance. And frankly, who can blame the poor thing for howling? Nearly every reported sighting you come across starts off with, 'I was out hunting…'

Being shot at does have a tendency to stress the already vulnerable breeding population. Although the fact that these animals are not recognised by the authorities as real can be a great benefit to the average cryptid owner, the downside to this is that they are afforded very little protection in law.

As a result, many howlers seem to have thought, 'Sod this for a game of soldiers,' and promptly moved on, choosing to make their homes not out in the wilds, but instead by urban firesides.

Like most felines, the howlers have a real knack for finding welcoming homes…or at least for finding homes. They don't really care if they are welcome or not. This is the nature of cats, and you should feel honoured if one chooses to set up home with you. You will be required to provide food and shelter, and there'll be none of that living outside nonsense – it will take the best chair by the fire, and will expect you to be its loyal slave, and be damn well happy about it, too.

In return, you will be allowed tummy-tickling privileges, and if you are very lucky the howler will purr softly as you stroke it.

They do make excellent family pets and will happily play with a ball of string, or if you have one of those little laser-light pens they will go absolutely crazy for it.

You will need a larger than average cat flap. In fact you may as well just leave the door open. They are not really aware of just how large they are, and do have a tendency to get stuck halfway through standard cat flaps.

Although this may initially strike you as hilarious, please remember that, like any feline, the howler values its dignity and will not be best pleased to find you laughing, or filming it for *You've Been Framed*. At this point you may well discover that lurking beneath its fluffy exterior are razor-sharp teeth and claws, and an equally razor-sharp temper.

It is well known that domestic cats will, on occasion, deposit a dead mouse on the doorstep as a token of their love for you – or at least as a way of saying that they are prepared to tolerate you. The howler has been known to demonstrate similar behavioural traits, but you have to scale this up in accordance with their larger size. So, don't be surprised if you find things like dead sheep and cows on the doorstep along with your morning paper. Just something to bear in mind.

If you do decide to home one of these little cuties you will never again have to worry about stray dogs wandering into your garden…or other cats…or sheep…or buffalo…or salespeople.

EATS	Fresh fish and poultry – and it's not too fussed about whether this is the stuff you have bought at the supermarket or stuff it has found for itself in next-door's kitchen…or next-door's fish pond. It will also drink the milk from your breakfast cereal, and is really not concerned with trivialities like whether or not you had actually *finished* with it.
LIKES	As with all felines, it likes to be adored. Indeed it *expects* to be adored, and woe betide you if you don't get the adoring right.
DISLIKES	Being chastised for playfully eviscerating the local wildlife. Any cat person knows this is only done in fun and no real harm was ever intended.

BROSNO DRAGON

IN TRUTH, THIS CREATURE IS MORE OF A GIANT SEA SERPENT THAN A DRAGON. FOUND IN LAKE BROSNO IN RUSSIA, IT IS KNOWN TO THE LOCALS AS BROSNYA, WHICH IS REALLY RATHER A PRETTY, ALBEIT INCONGRUOUS, NAME FOR AN ANIMAL THAT IS SAID TO HAVE SWALLOWED A GERMAN WARPLANE WHOLE SOME YEARS AGO.

In fact, this is a somewhat dubious story, as sea serpents are known to be shy and reclusive creatures (otherwise they would have their photos plastered all over the tabloids on a regular basis, and wouldn't qualify as cryptozoological creatures at all). In addition to this, their dietary needs tend to consist of small marine animals and fish; and only very rarely can warplanes be considered to fall into either category.

Theories on the existence and categorisation of Brosnya tend to fall into two basic camps. The first states that this is a terrible and ferocious sea monster which, in addition to snacking on military hardware, has also developed a taste for people, horses, and just about any other unwary creature that may venture near the water's edge. The second camp states that this is all a bunch of baloney, and it's probably just swamp gas. The second camp, however, are careful not to pitch their tents too close to the water, just in case.

The truth, as is so often the case, is much less exotic. The Brosno dragon is actually quite a timid creature on the whole, living a solitary existence away from the glare of publicity. Although these animals are hatched in groups, they mature quickly and then go off in search of their own territory, and generally go to some considerable lengths to avoid contact with others of their species until the mating season.

As with so many creatures, the mating season, which lasts only a few weeks in the summer, begins with the ritual of dancing around their handbags (although in the case of the Brosno dragon a crocodile handbag may well still be in the form of a crocodile – indeed, it may even still be *alive*).

Despite its somewhat fearsome reputation, the only time that any prospective owner need be wary of the Brosno dragon is during the mating season, or when there is a dispute over territory. Time things just right and you can nip in and grab a handful of unhatched eggs to take home and rear as your own. Time things just wrong and you will end up as dinner.

EATS	Just about anything it wants to, including scrap metal, and even metal that was still being used and was perfectly good for a few more years, thank you very much.
LIKES	Reading. Quilting. Cross-stitch.
DISLIKES	Call centres.

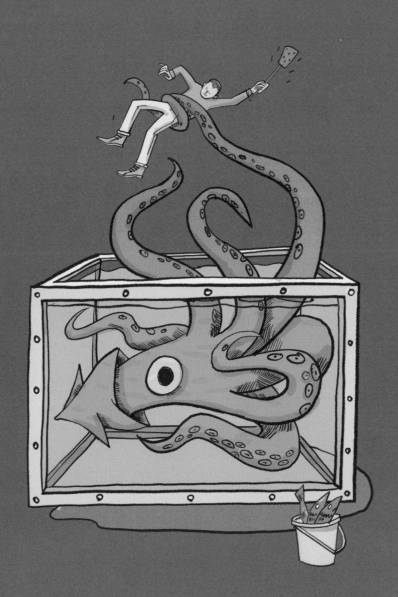

KRAKEN

Don't let the pet shop owner convince you this one will be happy living in a little goldfish bowl on the sideboard. This animal needs space.

It also needs hugs. This is demonstrated in many old mariners' drawings of the large majestic kraken stretching its tentacles around a passing ship. They are really just looking for love.

BOGEYMAN

THIS ONE FALLS NOT SO MUCH UNDER THE HEADING
OF CRYPTOZOOLOGY AS IT DOES PERHAPS FOLKLORE
AND MYTHOLOGY. NEVERTHELESS. IT IS ONE OF THOSE
CREATURES THAT WE. INSTINCTIVELY. JUST KNOW IS REAL.

The bogeyman is somewhat difficult to categorise since, being
created essentially from fear, its shape is dictated by the nature
of that fear. Hence, if your greatest fear when you turn off your
bedside light is of a faceless monster oozing slime and dripping
blood, then that is what you will get. Similarly, if you fear a glistening
pile of uncut diamonds, then that is how your particular bogeyman
will appear.

That's the theory, anyway, but since no one has yet been found
who has a pathological fear of suddenly becoming rich, and who

also happens to sleep with the light off in a room full of dark and mysterious shadows, then it remains to this day, only a theory.

Bogeymen, in general, are quite shy creatures, which is the *real* reason they tend to hide under the bed or behind the door. Unfortunately, this is often mistaken for 'lurking menacingly' under the bed or behind the door, and hence the poor bogeyman, as a species, has acquired an unnecessarily negative reputation.

Parents have historically used the threat of the bogeyman to scare naughty children into behaving, by saying that the creature is hiding in the shadows, waiting to attack any child who is foolish enough to stay awake. This shows a very confused sort of logic, as surely if the bogeyman really was the type of monster who attacks naughty children, it would be just as likely to attack a sleeping child as one who is sitting up in bed playing on an iPhone and plotting ways to burn down the garden shed.

In fact, the bogeyman is a benign soul, who for some reason seeks out the company of human children, but then is usually too nervous to actually communicate with them.

The mature bogeyman has a unique talent for shape-shifting. This explains why so few are seen. Once they realise someone is looking at them they will transform into an innocent lampshade, or a cuddly toy apparently discarded on the floor. The young bogeyman, however, tends to have less success in this area, and often transforms into something completely inappropriate, such as a plate of chocolate éclairs, which is just the sort of thing that would appeal to a naughty child who is reluctant to go to sleep. Many young bogeymen are lost in this way.

Bogeymen are an endangered species, and trade in them is forbidden under current laws. It is quite permissible, however, to create your own. Do ensure you carry a baseball bat, or some other suitable weapon, just in case your fear creates a particularly scary bogeyman. Once you have beaten it into submission, you will find it a playful and loving companion, requiring very little in the way of feeding and grooming. Bogeymen cease to exist in daylight, but if you treat them with kindness they will spontaneously reincarnate themselves each evening at dusk, just in time for a quick game of Monopoly before bed.

EATS	Naughty children (in fact, there are no recorded instances of bogeymen actually eating children of any persuasion, but the myth that they do has proven particularly stubborn, and the legal department have insisted, therefore, that 'naughty children' should be included here). They are also partial to chocolate-covered marshmallows.
LIKES	Board games, but only if you let them win.
DISLIKES	Bright lights. People with baseball bats.

FELINE BIPEDS

Feline bipeds? Seriously?? As if cats weren't cocky enough already – now they're walking around on two legs? They'll be wanting mobile phones next.

BEAR LAKE MONSTER

IT IS WIDELY ACKNOWLEDGED THAT WATCHING FISH SWIM AROUND CAN HELP PEOPLE RELAX, AS IS EVIDENCED BY THE FREQUENCY WITH WHICH AQUARIUMS ARE FOUND IN DENTISTS' WAITING ROOMS.

(As if *that's* going to calm you down while you're waiting for your root canal).

If you are one of those people who find solace in watching aquatic creatures weave their way around bits of seaweed and fake sunken treasure, but you yearn for the mystique of a more exotic animal, then the Bear Lake Monster could well be the one for you. Mind you, you will need an exceptionally large fish tank.

Found predominantly in Bear Lake in Utah (which rather takes the mystery out of its name, don't you think?), this is one of the larger serpents. It is quite a shy creature, long and thin like a snake, with ears sticking out of its skinny head – although some rather dubious sources describe it as wearing sunglasses and a baseball cap, but it is likely they are describing its more publicity-hungry cousin, the Bear Lake novelty ferry, which is happy to be photographed with both tourists and locals alike.

Some reports state that the Bear Lake monster has short legs, which make it look quite ungainly as it scurries about on land, yet in the water it is a veritable speed machine. Properly trained, this animal could save enthusiastic water-skiers an absolute fortune in boat-hire fees.

EATS	Mostly seafood. People (given half a chance).
LIKES	Scuba divers.
DISLIKES	Wetsuits – it's too hard to get the wrapper off.

FLATHEAD LAKE MONSTER

A distant cousin of Nessie, living in Flathead Lake in Montana – from the side of the family we don't talk to any more, since that business at Uncle Albert's funeral.

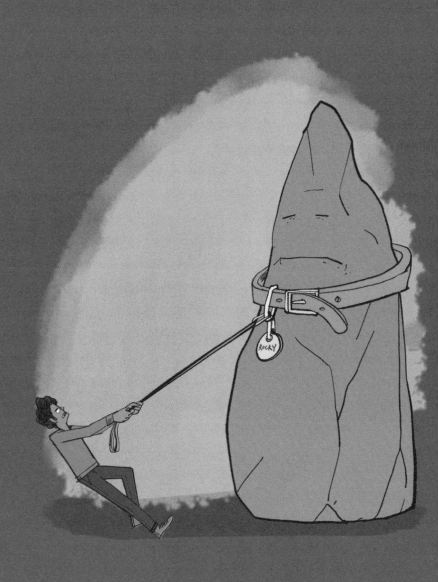

STANDING STONES

Perhaps not the best choice for those with an active lifestyle, but at least you will always have a pretty good idea where your pet is.

You know how sometimes you may have a little puppy who doesn't actually want to go for a walk, and he just freezes up and refuses to move? Well, it's a bit like that with standing stones, except that you are at a significant disadvantage as no amount of tugging on the lead will persuade it to move if it *really* doesn't want to.

CRYPTIDS
FOR THE
WILD-EYED
ADVENTURER

WITH A TASTE FOR EXCITEMENT AND A
TOTAL DISREGARD FOR PERSONAL SAFETY·

AHOOL

THIS IS DEFINITELY NOT ONE FOR THE BEGINNER.
YOU COULD TRY WORKING YOUR WAY UP THROUGH
CROCODILES AND TIGERS, AND ONCE YOU HAVE MASTERED
THOSE, AND MANAGED TO KEEP ALL YOUR LIMBS INTACT,
MAYBE THEN YOU WILL BE READY FOR THE AHOOL.

The ahool, in simple terms, is a large bat. But in reality it's so much more than that. Sporting a 12ft wingspan and a body the size of a small child, its most notable feature is probably the large claws on its forearms. Imagine one of these hurtling towards you as you stand, arms outstretched, calmly holding out a piece of herring for it to nibble on. Fish fingers would do, too, but it's as well to defrost them first.

The ahool has a flattened face, grey fur, and large black eyes. It doesn't take Mulder and Scully to work out that the ahool may well be responsible for the many sightings of so-called 'grey' aliens in

recent times, as it peers forlornly into bedroom windows, vainly hoping to be allowed back indoors.

Imaginatively named for its distinctive cry, 'A-hool, a-hool, a-hool', it has been cursed by the same sort of uninspired thinking as that shown by the bright spark who decided to call the orange an orange, instead of, say, a 'tangy pucker fruit'. Call yours something more original, like George or Fred.

The ahool is native to the island of Java, but can be imported easily without any of that messy paperwork, as it can simply fly over to your chosen country, and will be willing to follow a trail of fish just about anywhere.

The ahool does take quite a lot of looking after, however, and is generally considered to be a relatively high-maintenance pet. It will need to be exercised daily, or preferably nightly, as it is a nocturnal animal. If you live within flying distance of a freshwater lake you could try just letting it out each evening, but make sure you leave an upstairs window open for its return.

They are not the brightest of animals, but they are fiercely loyal to just about anyone who gives them fish, so you should have no fear of it wandering too far off. Being so much larger than the average bat it will, naturally, require a particularly high perch to hang from when sleeping, and would be ideally suited to life in a high-rise apartment.

Here is what to do if you are faced with an ahool hurtling towards you at speed with a hungry glint it its eyes:

Stay calm.
Breathe.
Raise your whole (fully defrosted) herring high up in the air.
Brace yourself.
Pray.

Here is what to do if you are faced with an ahool hurtling towards you at speed with a hungry glint it its eyes, and you are fresh out of herring:

Run.

The ahool is known for its playful nature, and would make a fantastic choice of pet for the more adventurous among us – those who enjoy extreme sports, for example, or who are experienced in activities such as bungee-jumping and hang-gliding. It is essential that you have a calm and cool disposition, and will not be prone to screaming wildly and waving your arms about if your pet chooses to wrestle playfully with you, or attempts to carry you from the window of your tenth-floor flat to the local canal. This is merely an attempt at bonding and shows that you have finally won its trust.

You will find head-to-toe padded clothing a useful addition to your wardrobe, and these items can often be purchased at generous discounts from former police dog trainers.

EATS	Fresh fish. Fish fingers. Fish sticks. Occasionally may take a bite out of someone who doesn't let go of the fish soon enough.
LIKES	Fishing.
DISLIKES	Frozen fish. Fish in tins.

HOWLER MONKEY SNAKE

In fact, this isn't a snake at all, it's a mammal that simply happens to look a bit like a snake on first glance. Actually, most of the people who see it don't *get* a second glance, so no one is really sure exactly what it looks like.

It is known to have a voracious appetite and can swallow its victims whole…including humans. Most sightings go something like this:

'Oh look, a howler monkey sn…aaaaarrrrggghhhhhh!!!!!!!'

If you are of an adventurous disposition and feel this animal would suit your lifestyle, you will first need to locate one in the wild. No one has successfully survived long enough to set up and operate any kind of stud farm, so it is not believed that there are any examples of this species in captivity and you will have to go to Brazil to find one.

The next consideration (putting aside the challenges you may encounter in trying to transport this animal), is where you will house it.

This is a lake-dwelling creature that can grow up to 18ft long. If you are not fortunate enough to have your own private lake, you may consider releasing it into any large nearby body of water.

The resulting sightings are bound to increase the tourist activity in your region, and the occasional disappearance is surely a reasonable price to pay. After all, if people are going to wander about close to the water's edge they've really only got themselves to blame.

DOBHAR-CHU

Many people visit Ireland for the fishing. The dobhar-chu might provide just the incentive they need to get a grip and find a more relaxing hobby, like BASE-jumping or snake-wrangling.

Also known as Doyarchu or the Irish crocodile, this animal is often described as being half-dog, half-otter, and half mad as hell. Yes, I know the maths doesn't add up, but who can do arithmetic properly when being dragged into the water by a bloodthirsty aquatic mammal?

In a word: avoid!

CHEMOSIT
(AKA CHIMISET, CHIMISIT, CHIMOSIT)

Not quite your average hairy bipedal ape. This chap is to be found in Kenya, and to be frank, is probably best left there. The hard man's answer to Bigfoot; not one for viewers of a nervous disposition. Angry, vicious and downright ill-mannered.

On the surface, this creature is not entirely dissimilar to Bigfoot, but this one has definite anger-management issues. Experts believe the breed as a whole suffers from a massive inferiority complex – most likely due to the fact that no one seems to know how to spell its name. This may seem like a minor issue, but incorrect use of vowels is a serious matter, and it will cause you endless problems when it comes to filling out the insurance forms if it should choose to bite one of your guests…which it probably will.

ARABHAR

FOUND AROUND THE ARABIAN SEA, THIS MYSTERIOUS
FLYING SNAKE REMAINS UNRECOGNISED AS AN OFFICIAL
SPECIES, AND THEREIN LIES THE GREAT ATTRACTION.

Flying snakes are, of course, nothing new. There are a number of different species recorded, and it is easy enough to find information about their life and habits. But anyone can own a flying snake of a *known* species. Where's the fun in that?

The arabhar, like other flying snakes, lives in trees and 'flies' between the branches. In fact, it doesn't actually have wings and cannot truly fly, nor do anything remotely aerobatic. It simply flattens its body, and basically floats between the trees in much the same way that crocodiles don't. It's really little more than optimistic falling.

They are quite lively, playful creatures and have been known to bite on rare occasions. Well, OK, not really *rare* occasions. Well, all right, quite a lot, actually.

It should be noted that, although the bite is venomous, this does not cause too much of a problem to humans…well, only to those particularly sensitive individuals. The venom is really only strong enough to harm the small vertebrates that make up the main part of the arabhar's diet, and frankly if you're going to complain about a few crippling stomach cramps, oozing sores and short-term blindness then perhaps you shouldn't be looking to home an exotic pet in the first place.

To be on the safe side, it is probably best not to home one of these if you have other pets, or small children. In short, they do not make especially good domestic pets, and do require a considerable amount of special care, such as a large vertical tank containing lots of branches, and a permanently humid environment.

Of course, if the outside temperature rises to the arabhar's range of tolerance then you can allow your pet to roam the house freely, but do ensure your liability insurance covers you for unexpected attacks on any visitors. It is also recommended that you are careful when reaching out for the handrail on your stairs, as this particular household fixture seems to remind them of the trees in their native region, and they have been known to wrap themselves around the banister and lie in wait for any unsuspecting fingers which may come their way.

CHUPACABRA

THIS ONE, IT HAS TO BE ADMITTED, HAS SOMETHING OF AN IMAGE PROBLEM. IT HAS TO BE FURTHER ADMITTED THAT THIS ISN'T ENTIRELY UNJUSTIFIED.

The famous 'goat-sucker' found primarily in Mexico and Puerto Rico, the chupacabra has been blamed for the mysterious deaths of numerous goats, cattle and other livestock, found with puncture wounds and apparently drained of blood.

The earliest descriptions of this animal say it has spines down its back and glowing red eyes. It hops like a kangaroo, smells of sulphur and has three toes. There are even suggestions that it may not be a native of this planet.

Theories range from it being livestock that escaped from a crashed UFO, through to it being a genetic experiment that escaped from a secret government laboratory.

It's not the cuddliest of creatures, and to be honest, with the amount of negative press it has received, you can't entirely blame it for having a bit of an attitude problem. Who wouldn't be a tad miffed at seeing themselves pilloried and vilified every time they pick up a newspaper?

More recently, however, the chupacabra has undergone something of a makeover, and has begun a tour of the USA – where it is described as basically a cross-bred coyote with mange, and has even been caught on film. Pretty good public relations there: the spin doctors certainly earned their money in taking this animal from a blood-sucking alien freak to a hybrid dog with a skin problem.

Experienced cryptozoologists are not fooled by this, which is clearly a government-managed media campaign designed to convince the public at large that there is really nothing to worry about.

If you are in this for the kudos you will most definitely want to stick with the pure-bred, red-eyed chupacabra (which has most definitely *not* been so indiscreet as to allow itself to be caught on film), even if it is a little more risky – indeed, perhaps *because* it is a little more risky.

This is an animal for the more adventurous owner, someone who likes to live dangerously and isn't afraid of evisceration. But only in fun. Well, probably only in fun…Well, to be perfectly honest it's sometimes hard to tell the difference between playfulness and apoplectic rage.

Given the volatile nature of this species, the chupacabra is probably not the best choice of cryptid if you have young children or other pets, but with the right training this one would be absolutely ideal for getting rid of doorstep salesmen…or the window cleaner… or your best friend who just popped round with your birthday present…or indeed anyone else who dares contemplate an approach to your property.

A number of owners maintain that the chupacabra can be trained quite easily with the aid of a whistle and a few boxes of dog kibble.

Others are less skilled in this area and some have even been known to resort to electric shocks as a training method. There is, understandably, some debate about the ethics of using electric collars (frankly, if you can't take a little playful exsanguination from time to time, you probably shouldn't be in this game in the first place) and the Breeders' Association has recently voted to blacklist any owner found to be using such a device.

Dog kibble it is, then.

Some owners, however, still feel that the collar is the only sure-fire way to avoid being disembowelled in the night, and so stick rigidly to their guns…often, in fact, sleeping with one under the pillow and fully loaded just on the off-chance that their chupacabra should prove particularly resistant to domestication.

EATS	Goats. Actually not the whole goat, just the blood – it's on a diet and counting calories.
LIKES	Jumping out of the shadows and randomly attacking people in the dead of night.
DISLIKES	Newspapers. TV documentaries. People. Cars. Shops. Peanuts. Dog collars. Traffic lights. Pretty much everything.

WENDIGO

Generally considered as little more than legend, and falling under the category of folklore rather than honest-to-goodness cryptozoology, the wendigo is basically a 12ft-tall, stick-thin humanoid.

They are always hungry and look extremely emaciated, with bones showing through the skin. For this reason, it was once thought that they would make excellent high-fashion models. Indeed, there was a brief trend for using the wendigo as a working animal in this way, and the sight of a wendigo flouncing down a catwalk in the latest *haute couture* is certainly something to behold, but since their preferred food is human beings, the flouncing up and down the catwalk only lasted about an hour before they got peckish and…let's just say it didn't end well.

The wendigo is extremely long-lived, so this is a serious commitment on your part if you choose to home one. That said, you probably won't have to worry about looking after it for very long as you will be eaten pretty quickly, and then it will be someone else's problem.

Some people think it is possible to domesticate the wendigo, but none have survived to tell us exactly *how* this can be done. The only advice I can offer is if you see your pet reaching for a knife and fork…run!

HONEY ISLAND SWAMP MONSTER

This has all the makings of a brilliant horror film. We have the monster itself, which on the whole sounds like a distant relative of Bigfoot, but is said to be a cross between a chimp and a crocodile (which seems a bit of an odd combination, even for a low-budget B-movie), and then we have the conspiracy theory – which is where it *really* gets interesting.

Basically, the story goes like this…the monster was seen (naturally only by one or two people, who – somewhat predictably – just happened *not* to have a camera with them at the time), plaster casts were made of spooky three-toed monster footprints, mass panic ensued, influx of media, tourist industry poised to open a string of souvenir shops. Everything looking good, and then, all of a sudden, before it really even got off the ground, the whole thing was exposed as a hoax – apparently just some guy walking around with carefully constructed 'monster footprint' shoes.

Frankly, this was rather a disappointing turn of events for those in the cryptozoology community, many of whom felt jolly cross about the whole thing.

The story of the hoax was then launched to the media with all the hoo-ha of the latest red-carpet première, and much publicity was given to the monster-print shoes.

And that, apparently, was that. Mystery solved.

Well…erm…perhaps not.

Frankly, the exposé wasn't all that convincing and conspiracy theorists have been quick to question the validity of the hoax claims. After all, if the fake shoes that were supposedly used to make the tracks have four long toes, how come the footprint plaster casts show three toes and webbed feet?

Clearly this is definitive proof that the animal is *real*, and the exposé itself is merely a hastily concocted cover story. As is to be expected in these situations, many people will be taken in by the cover story, after all governments never lie to their citizens, do they?

The truly dedicated, however, will continue searching in the hope that, one day, this poor forlorn creature may be brought into the warmth and safety of the cryptozoology community's collective bosom.

CRYPTIDS FOR THE ETERNAL OPTIMIST

WHO WON'T ACCEPT THAT HIS PET
IS SIMPLY WAITING FOR THE RIGHT
OPPORTUNITY TO EAT HIM.

MAN-EATING TREE

Next we look at the ongoing and rather heated debate about the classification of the man-eating tree. Some consider this to be just flora, albeit flora of an unusual and somewhat reckless persuasion, while others posit the theory that it is a real, flesh-and-blood animal, which simply masquerades as a tree in order to lure its prey.

Such concerns will probably matter little to you if you are simply looking to home a cuddly and affectionate pet, but if you wish to register as a trainer or breeder, then it will become necessary to decide where you stand. Either way, it is not recommended that you stand too close to this magnificent yet playful beast.

KALANORO

THIS IS A BIPEDAL APE WITH A DIFFERENCE… ACTUALLY WITH QUITE A FEW DIFFERENCES.

Perhaps the most remarkable thing about this animal is its three-toed feet, not because of the number of toes but because of the general orientation of the foot itself, which faces backwards. Quite how this feature evolved is not known, but it does confer a clear evolutionary advantage in that the backwards-facing feet make the animal extremely difficult to track. A number of dedicated cryptozoologists have spent many days tracking kalanoro footprints in the wilds of Madagascar, only to find out where it had previously *been*, rather than where it was going.

Aside from this one little quirk, dress it in jogging bottoms and a hoodie, and the kalanoro could probably get by pretty much unnoticed on virtually any street corner, although it does have longer than average fingers, large eyes, and quills along its back. This unusual feature is also seen in the chupacabra – although the two are not thought to be related, and it is supposed that this is merely an example of convergent evolution.

This animal does not make a particularly good pet. It looks just human enough for it to be awkward if you try to tickle its tummy – and in any case it is known for its aggressive temperament, and inability to take a joke. Another thing it is known for is abducting children…but it's generally happy enough to give them back in exchange for food.

Nevertheless, this type of behaviour is simply not acceptable in polite society and frankly it's likely to get you thrown out of the golf club if it should get around that your pet has been kidnapping kiddies. The authorities do not take kindly to people in hoodies hanging around outside schools these days.

My guess is the kalanoros haven't met the Year 7s from the local comprehensive, or they would think twice about abducting anyone.

EATS	Children…possibly. Best not to take any chances.
LIKES	Schools.
DISLIKES	Chupacabras – the kalanoro were the first to evolve spine quills and they do not appreciate their innovation being copied. Plus the chupacabra gets much worse publicity and the kalanoros don't see why they should take the stick for sucking the blood out of dead cattle when they are absolutely innocent of this and only suck the blood out of children. Erm…that is, they are absolutely innocent. End of.

LIZARD MEN

There have always been reports of strange bipedal reptiles lurking around swampland, the most famous of which is probably the lizard man of Scape Ore Swamp in the USA, which has been blamed for a number of attacks, mainly on vehicles.

Even if you do happen to own your own swamp, this animal is not recommended for domestication. It is violent and aggressive, and does not respond well to conventional training methods.

In fact, this one probably shouldn't even be considered a cryptid as such. If certain conspiracy theories are to be believed, the lizard men have been here longer than we have. They think of this as their planet and *we* are the interlopers.

Clearly, from the reports of lizard men attacking people and cars, there is some division within lizard society. We must assume that the ones making the news are the outcasts, the uneducated, the simple-minded. The attacks are more than likely a result of the anger felt by these lizards at no longer being afforded the respect and power which is held by others of their species.

Yes, that's right – power. Any conspiracy theorist worth his salt knows about the lizard masters and the secret way in which they control everything that happens in our society (and have done since they contrived the demise of the other dinosaurs who refused to capitulate…that asteroid 65 million years ago didn't just happen by all on its own, y'know).

FAIRY/FAERIE

It's a common misconception that 'faerie' is just a more mystical spelling of 'fairy', and that the two are, in fact, the same creature. Some people, quite erroneously, think the difference only matters to etymologists and spelling geeks. Nothing could be further from the truth.

Fairies are nice and dainty and live at the bottom of your garden. They are only visible to children, and are thoroughly wonderful creatures (think tooth fairy, flower fairy etc.). They are not to be confused with the more sinister 'faerie' (note spelling – this has been adopted to denote that they are altogether more devious and sinister than your average tooth fairy).

These are not the type to sit around waiting patiently for your tooth to fall out of its own accord. No, they are much more likely to attack you in the dead of night with a pair of pliers. We are talking roadworks faerie, doggie-doo-doo faerie, cash-machine-that-eats-your-credit-card faerie, that type of thing. Be warned.

ETHIOPIAN DEATH BIRD

A BIT OF AN UNFORTUNATE NAME, REALLY. I MEAN, HOW CAN PEOPLE BE EXPECTED TO WARM TO AN ANIMAL CALLED A 'DEATH BIRD'?

Actually, it isn't even a bird. This is a really cute little bat, with the most adorable face you could possibly imagine on a blood-sucking vampire.

The death bird does have something of an image problem, however. This is primarily due to its habit of drinking blood, but if you're really honest about it, what pet doesn't have the odd little behavioural quirk?

Pound for pound, you won't find a more loving and affectionate pet. As long as you don't plan on touring the local schools with it, or visiting crowded shopping centres, you should be just fine.

The death bird loves human company and will 'purr' when stroked. They do love to nuzzle…you may want to switch to wearing turtle-neck jumpers just to be on the safe side, though.

EATS	Erm...well...blood. Pretty much just blood. Yep, exclusively blood. Oh, and peanuts. It likes peanuts, too. But mainly blood.
LIKES	People who are trusting and like to nuzzle, and who generally don't wear turtle-neck jumpers.
DISLIKES	Turtle-neck jumpers.

JERSEY DEVIL

ON FIRST HEARING THE NAME YOU WERE PROBABLY THINKING OF THOSE IRRITATING LITTLE FABRIC FLUFF BOBBLES THAT MYSTERIOUSLY POP UP ALL OVER YOUR FAVOURITE TOP AFTER IT'S BEEN THROUGH THE WASHING MACHINE A FEW TIMES.

If so, you can heave a big sigh of relief and relax, because the real Jersey devil is nowhere near as bad as that.

A minimal amount of research will tell you that the Jersey devil is a 7ft-tall winged biped with a horse-like head and rather appealing glowing red eyes. It is also known to have a human-like scream.

And just *how* do we know this? Because people keep attacking the poor thing! In fact, this animal has to be one of the most persecuted of all the cryptids.

It is actually a shy and reclusive animal but occasionally people do catch a glimpse of it and then, quite inexplicably, start throwing things at it or even shooting at it. Just because a mysterious 7ft-tall bipedal animal with wings, hooves and glowing red eyes happens to leap out at you in the woods, this is no excuse for violence.

The Jersey devil is considered by many to be a pest, and these people have convinced themselves, quite wrongly, that it needs to be culled. It is now an endangered species due to the growing pastime of devil hunting, in which hordes of bloodthirsty middle-management team-builders group together from all across the globe to charge through the woods chasing after it with big sticks.

This approach is really not compatible with ongoing conservation efforts, and has had a detrimental impact on the animal's habitat and numbers. Indeed, it is believed there are very few specimens left in the wild and the breeding population has been severely compromised due to the thoughtless actions of these hunters.

Thankfully, there is a captive-breeding programme in operation, hidden somewhere in deepest Wigan (UK). This has been operating for almost two years now, and conservationists are hopeful that young Jersey devils may shortly be released back into the wild.

If you feel this might be a suitable pet for you, it is recommended that you take in a breeding pair if at all possible, as concerns remain about the viability of this species.

EATS	Mostly cheeseburgers and fries.
LIKES	People – this animal is really very affectionate and just wants to be loved.
DISLIKES	People who chase about in the woods at night waving big sticks.

YOWIE

This hairy bipedal ape is not entirely dissimilar to Bigfoot – but this is Bigfoot with an antipodean twist.

During the warm Australian summers this poor creature suffers terribly from prickly heat and is tormented by midges. He does look a sight in his little hat with the corks dangling from the brim – but you are advised not to snigger as the heat only aggravates his bad temper, and having your arm ripped out of its socket may offend.

WEREWOLF

IF YOU ARE THINKING OF HOMING A WEREWOLF,
YOU PROBABLY ALREADY KNOW A LITTLE BIT ABOUT THE
SPECIES, SUCH AS THE EFFECT OF LUNAR ACTIVITY ON
THEIR BEHAVIOUR, AND THE USEFULNESS OF KEEPING
A STOCK OF SILVER BULLETS JUST IN CASE THE
LUNAR ACTIVITY GETS OUT OF HAND.

You probably also know that a significant number of werewolves
don't actually *know* that they are werewolves, and as a result can
suffer from stress and anxiety if, on waking, they find themselves
with bloodstained hands and the remains of livestock scattered
about the room. It is not recommended that you bother with this
type of werewolf as they are very hard work and, frankly, the cost of
the psychiatric help they need is prohibitive.

Your best bet is to go for the ones who know exactly what they
are, and who are actually quite comfortable with it. They are easily

domesticated and can make very loving pets, as long as you take a few simple precautions like boarding up the windows in accordance with the phases of the moon, not leaving them alone with the children, that sort of thing.

Many people are drawn to dogs as pets because of their loyal, playful nature. They give you unconditional love and are always happy and excited to see you. Please do not fall into the trap of thinking that a werewolf is simply an exotic breed of dog. Yes, it *is* an exotic pet, and there is certainly kudos to be gained from owning one, but your average werewolf is a tad more cynical.

While in human form they generally have little or no memory of their time in wolf form, but they *do* retain some residual memory on a subconscious level, and while they may not know exactly *why*, they will still view you with contempt because of all those times you danced like no one was watching and completely forgot that the werewolf was curled up in his bed gazing at you with a perplexed expression on his face.

This residual memory works the other way, too, and this makes them very difficult to train. While a dog may be happy to sit on command, a werewolf will have a vague memory of once having been the one *giving* the commands and therefore will not take kindly to being asked to roll over or beg for table scraps.

The werewolf may *appear* to be content with playing fetch and chasing rabbits, but it should not be confused with a dog.

Much like vampires, werewolves are enjoying a resurgence in popular culture these days. Well, perhaps 'enjoying' isn't quite the right word, as they are generally quite secretive about the wolf side of their persona. Many thinkers believe they have their own agenda, and while no one is entirely sure of what this agenda is, it is wise to treat the species with caution.

It is well known that if you are bitten by a werewolf you will very likely become one yourself. The reason for this side-effect is not yet fully understood, but it does suggest there is a desire to increase their numbers, and some have theorised that they work a bit like the Borg in *Star Trek*, and are actually assimilating people into their species as part of a dark and sinister plot to take over the world.

Do not let this put you off homing a werewolf, however. It is probably good insurance to pamper it and lavish it with the best toys and the most luxurious bedding…then when the revolution comes your pet may feel more inclined to protect you from the others in the werewolf uprising. Just something to bear in mind.

EATS	Dog kibble, livestock, people (not necessarily in that order). It's a little-known fact that they also love chocolate ice cream.
LIKES	Moonlit walks.
DISLIKES	Silver bullets…and people who keep a sneaky supply of silver bullets hidden in the house – it's almost as if you don't trust them.

MAMLAMBO

Given that this very, very long crocodile-type animal is also known as the 'brain sucker' it is worth asking if this is a suitable choice of pet for owners of a nervous disposition.

You could try obedience classes, but make sure you keep a list of local hospitals with an A&E department, just on the off chance that the obedience classes don't work.

It has been suggested (not by me, of course) that this is perhaps an ideal pet for those employed in middle management, since they don't appear to use their brains anyway.

KAPPA

ROUGHLY THE SAME SIZE AS A HUMAN CHILD, AND
SIMILARLY WELL KNOWN FOR LEAVING SLIMY FOOTPRINTS
ALL OVER THE HOUSE, THE KAPPA HAS ACQUIRED A BIT
OF A REPUTATION AS A TROUBLEMAKER.

Should you decide to home one of these river imps, you will need
to look carefully at the dietary requirements of the kappa, which
has been known to eat people…just occasionally, and only in fun,
nothing to worry about really.

And anyway, they actually prefer to eat cucumber, so if you have an
allotment you should be just fine.

Probably.

CRYPTIDS
AS COMPANION
ANIMALS

FOR THOSE WHO HAVE STYLE,
SOPHISTICATION AND A BLOODY GOOD
FIRST AID KIT.

ZOMBIES

IN RECENT YEARS ZOMBIES HAVE BECOME A MAJOR PART OF POPULAR CULTURE, AND NOW FIND THEMSELVES INVITED TO ALL THE BEST PARTIES.

Despite the fact that they are generally portrayed in the movies as crazed, mindless, unthinking beings bent on killing for the sake of killing, and never quite having the intellect to question whether it might be better to just go paint-balling to let off steam instead, they have somehow acquired a reputation as cuddly, amusing creatures who are fun to have around and not really all that dangerous at all. This has led to a rise in the number of people wanting to home one.

The reality is that they do not make good household pets. They shed on the carpet, and keep you awake all night with their moaning. They are prone to moods and will try to kill you for no apparent reason.

In fact, many experts now suspect that the zombie is just incredibly pissed off at the fact that you are properly alive and afforded all the rights and privileges associated with such a condition, while they are, to put it bluntly, dead. Or at least undead – which, although it isn't quite the same as being dead, is even less the same as being alive.

Zombies, according to popular culture, like to eat brains. In fact, you will find they are equally happy with tofu, particularly if you can flavour it with a bit of garlic. Oh, and a little sprig of parsley would be nice to brighten up the presentation and make them feel valued.

In recent years there has been a move towards the 'show' zombie, and there is an annual competition held in Stockton-on-Tees (the UK zombie capital), where rosettes are awarded for Best in Breed and Obedience etc.

This is not without controversy, however, and even within the Zombie Appreciation Society there is much debate over the rights and wrongs of keeping zombies in a captive environment, and other important issues like whether having pink bows tied in their hair for the local Cutest Cryptid competition is degrading to zombies.

Some go even further and ask if the European Convention on Human Rights can reasonably be applied to the undead.

FLORIDA SKUNK APE

NOT MUCH TO TELL REALLY, THE NAME SAYS IT ALL. THIS IS AN APE, OR BIPEDAL PRIMATE, A NATIVE OF FLORIDA AND IT...ER...UM...WELL, TO BE BLUNT, IT HAS A SLIGHT PROBLEM WITH BODY ODOUR.

It has been suggested that the smells, rather than simply marking territory, are in fact used as a form of communication. Many people find the smell off-putting, so it's perhaps not the best choice if you have delicate olfactory senses, but it has to be said this pet is absolutely unrivalled for its ability to get rid of the in-laws quickly.

EATS	Goodness only knows what it eats, but it must be something pretty potent to produce a smell like that! You could try things like garlic or curry, as any resulting odours would be a positive improvement.
LIKES	People. Isn't it always the smelly pets that want to cuddle you?
DISLIKES	Air fresheners.

LAKE MONSTERS

THE TERM 'MONSTERS' IS USED HERE ONLY IN DEFERENCE TO POPULAR CULTURE, AND SHOULD NOT BE INTERPRETED AS HAVING ANYTHING WHATSOEVER TO DO WITH REALITY.

The vast majority of lake-dwelling serpents are actually gentle, playful creatures and are about as far removed from the proper definition of 'monsters' as it's possible to get. They don't abduct and murder people…they don't torture them…they don't clamp shoppers' cars when they only nipped into the corner shop for a pint of milk.

It is simply unacceptable to label these animals in this way, and it is this sort of blinkered attitude that has led to centuries of persecution of what is essentially a peaceful animal. The use of this kind of pejorative language suggests an inherent bias towards belief in all the adverse reporting, and frankly, if you refer to them in this way, you won't find any of the reputable breeders will be willing to let you home one of their animals.

There is a theory that most of the negative press is spread by those in the fishing industry who, rather than being afraid the serpent will eat *them*, are actually more concerned that it will eat the fish stocks and therefore cost them money. This persecution is based on economics, rather than on any physical threat.

OK, yes, there *have* been a handful of somewhat apocryphal reports of rogue serpents actually attacking small boats and the occasional swimmer. However, these reports are dismissed by experts as nothing more than the wild and fanciful ramblings of a few locals with over-active imaginations.

In fact, the serpents are well known for their playful nature, and just because they may have tried to climb into a boat once or twice this should not be interpreted as an act of aggression. It is merely the mischievous behaviour of an animal desperate for human interaction. Indeed, once on land they are known to adore board games, although they do tend to cheat if you don't keep a very close eye on them.

As is well documented, most sightings of lake monsters occur in areas where the lake is, or once was, connected to the sea. In many cases the 'lake monsters' are really just sea serpents who only became 'monsters' when their particular body of water became land-locked. There are some obvious exceptions to this rule, such as China's Lake Tianchi monster, which lives in a lake formed in a volcanic crater, with no apparent connection to the sea.

It would be a pretty dull world if everyone had the same tastes, as they say, and we must therefore assume that the serpent of Lake Tianchi simply doesn't like lazing on the beach with a knotted hanky on its head and an ice cream in its claws, and has chosen a more inland location instead.

There are many different sub-species of sea serpents found in various waters around the world – the marine equivalent of bigfoot/agogwe/yeti etc., etc., etc. As with exotic bipedal primates, it's really a simple case of choosing which one will best suit your lifestyle.

Treat these animals with respect, and your love will not go unrewarded as they will happily follow wherever you lead, and will adapt to virtually any region.

These are social animals, hunting and playing in groups. As such, it would really be unfair to separate them and it is recommended that you only consider a lake monster as a pet if your garden contains a large enough body of water in which to house an entire family group. This one is not really a suitable choice if you live in a high-rise apartment with limited space.

Should you decide to home a lake monster in your garden pond you will need to keep this information away from the local authorities or they will increase your council tax on the basis that you now have a swimming pool.

On the plus side, it's unlikely the local cats will have much interest in chasing your goldfish once they find out what else is living in your pond.

EATS	Small fish. Cheese and onion crisps. Small boats (but only in a very playful way).
LIKES	Lots of care and attention – this animal craves human company, but is painfully shy. This explains why most sightings are brief and vague as it usually turns and flees as soon as it realises it has been spotted.
DISLIKES	Cameras. Television documentary teams. Jumpers that really itch. Solitaire (these are truly social animals and they hate to play alone).

GIGLIOLI'S WHALE

Probably not the best choice for those who crave the kudos of owning a truly exotic pet.

Giglioli's whale is basically a perfectly normal whale in pretty much every respect, except that it has two dorsal fins instead of the more conventional single dorsal. This is a feature not seen in any other whale, and as a result, the scientists don't believe it's real.

Such a specific detail is unlikely to be noticed by your uninitiated friends, who will probably think that's just an ordinary everyday whale you have swimming about in a tank in your living room – and that, let's face it, is wholly unremarkable.

DODO

NOT (AS MANY PEOPLE SEEM TO BELIEVE) DEAD AT ALL. IN FACT
THE DODO HAS MERELY RETIRED FROM PUBLIC LIFE.

It hasn't been an easy journey for the dodo as a species. Initially
hunted almost to extinction, the dodo faked its own death in what
is widely regarded as a 'bloody good move'. Scientists are always
going on about how clever the crows are because they can use tools
(although admittedly, not power tools) to poke at insects etc., but
seriously that's nothing compared to the dodo.

The story of the dodo is, of course, well known. At least, the *end*
of the story is well known. What isn't so well known, however, is that
there are in fact two distinct species of dodo, the common 'luckless'
dodo and the lesser-spotted 'incognito' dodo.

Originally the two species were living happily together, sharing
the rent and stuff, everything was moving along nicely. Then
things changed quite suddenly when the two groups started having

'creative differences', possibly all boiling down to a silly argument over who ate the last of the breakfast cereal. Diplomatic relations were severed and in a startling display of divergent evolution the two groups split and went their separate ways.

A small number of remaining flocks of the common 'luckless' dodo adopted some unusual disguises in an effort to survive. Early efforts saw entire flocks of these birds disguising themselves as turkeys (sadly just before Christmas), or grouse (just as the shooting season was about to begin). Still others, of a more sea-faring bent, crept noiselessly in the night onto large vessels with exotic-sounding names like *Titanic* and *Mary Celeste*.

Some developed highly specialised diets and came to rely exclusively on the berries of a particular variety of bush, found growing only in certain isolated areas of Blackburn. Unfortunately once the land was sold for housing development their only food source was gone and that was pretty much it for the common dodo.

The lesser-spotted dodo fared slightly better, primarily as a result of its fearsome intelligence. It has managed to remain undetected for hundreds of years.

Unfortunately, when it comes to choosing a mate, the lesser-spotted dodo has become increasingly picky as the centuries roll by. Dodos of the opposite gender (although appearing to the impartial observer to be perfectly good choices as mates) are often deemed to have a beak that is slightly too long, or perhaps slightly too short. The legs are not quite the right colour, or the feathers just the wrong shade of cool. As a result even the lesser-spotted dodo has seen its numbers decline to unsustainable levels.

The dodo is now extremely rare and it is not recommended that any individuals be taken from the wild as this could stress the already vulnerable breeding population. Conservationists are currently working on a secret programme to reintroduce the dodo to parts of Cumbria, and they can get extremely uppity if they catch you trying to remove one of their tagged breeding birds. If you are able to source a captive-bred specimen, however, this is entirely acceptable.

NDENDEKI

This giant turtle from the Congo is a suitable choice as a pet or perhaps even as a working animal. Not only is this a loving pet to snuggle up with on cold winter evenings, but it can also double as a coffee table in an emergency.

CHESSIE

Nessie's American cousin – the one who always brings his old holiday photos to show everyone. This animal lives in Chesapeake Bay, but holidays pretty much anywhere there is water, so there are a LOT of holiday snaps to show around.

OGRE

Basically human in appearance, thick, brutish, and given to hanging around on street corners.

Actually, not as much fun as the media would have you believe. These guys have a taste for human flesh and seem to be in a permanent state of ire. Perhaps if they switched to lentil burgers they would develop a jollier outlook on life.

Fairly commonly found in popular culture so not really exotic enough to appeal to the true connoisseur. Anyway, looking so much like us, it would be a bit like putting a collar and lead on Uncle Hector and attempting to take him for a walk. No real kudos there, just some odd looks from passers-by.

WHITEY

WHITEY IS THE LOCAL NICKNAME FOR A SERPENT FOUND IN
THE WHITE RIVER AREA OF ARKANSAS, USA, WELL, MORE
ACTUALLY *IN* THE RIVER THAN THE SURROUNDING AREA.

This is one of the friendlier breeds of serpent and would make an
excellent family pet.

Unlike most of the animals mentioned here, however, ownership
of your own whitey is subject to various restrictions. A state
resolution was passed some time ago which makes it unlawful to
harm the animal. While many enthusiastic serpent owners would
not consider that giving this creature a loving home could in any
way constitute harming it, there is nevertheless some debate about
whether it is entirely legal to remove it from its native habitat. The
general consensus of opinion among cryptid owners is therefore that
this one should be avoided…unless you are able to source a private,
captive-bred, specimen.

It is rumoured that way back in the 1960s, before the resolution
was passed, a group of crazy, free-thinking hippies did manage to
capture a breeding pair and set up their own refuge. Naturally, it
would be imprudent to disclose the location, but if any interested
party were to check the free ads paper in somewhere like, say,
Hartlepool in the north-east of England, they might just be lucky
enough to find one on offer free to a good home. But you didn't hear
it from me.

CHAMP

Another one of Nessie's cousins – this one is from Lake Champlain in the USA. This *is* quite a large family group – something to bear in mind if you plan on inviting all the in-laws round for Christmas dinner.

CON RIT

Basically a centipede on steroids. If you are the type of person who runs screaming from a common-or-garden centipede that has inadvertently found its way into your bathtub, then you are unlikely to warm to this 60ft-long giant arthropod as a household companion – regardless of how cute it may be.

CRYPTIDS AS FAMILY PETS

BECAUSE THERE'S NO SUCH THING
AS TOO MUCH CHAOS.

SASQUATCH

THIS IS THE FLAGSHIP ANIMAL OF THE CRYPTIDS, THE FREE PACKET OF CRISPS SPAT OUT BY THE VENDING MACHINE OF LIFE.

This is the big one; the one that gets all the publicity – which is rather a shame really, because Bigfoot is actually quite a timid creature, traditionally going to great lengths to avoid publicity.

There are always some exceptions to any rule, and it is a little-known fact that Chewbacca in *Star Wars* is, in fact, a bigfoot.

And there is, of course, that one short piece of film shot by Roger Patterson and Bob Gimlin, which has caused so much controversy over the years. Is it a real bigfoot? Is it a man in a suit?

Various people have come forward and confessed to being the man in the suit, but none have been able to actually *prove* the claim, so the footage remains inconclusive.

Some have suggested it's more than likely that the film is a fake, pointing out that the real Bigfoot is far too reclusive, and far too *smart* to be found so easily out in the open (let's face it, Chewbacca had a very lucrative contract, but no such incentive has been recorded in the case of the Patterson-Gimlin film).

In fact, if you look closely at the film it is just possible to make out a real bigfoot peering out from behind a tree, clearly wondering what all the fuss is about.

Probably the most famous of all the exotic bipedal primates, bigfoot is the one most likely to make a good domestic pet or companion animal. They get on extremely well with other household pets and children.

The mature bigfoot grows to anything between 7ft and 10ft in height, so it would perhaps be better if you have one of those old Victorian homes with the high ceilings.

Native to various regions of North America and Canada, Bigfoot is a shy creature and it is often quite difficult to actually locate one in the wild. In fact, as they are considered an endangered species, going out into the wilderness to capture one is not recommended. This kind of activity can disrupt the fragile balance of the bigfoot community, and in any case a captive-bred bigfoot can be obtained with relative ease. There are a handful of registered breeders operating in America and Europe, and most will even house-train your pet for you.

Bigfoot is a gentle, sociable animal, possessed of some intelligence – although obviously it's not as intelligent as man, as is evidenced by the lack of guns, mobile phones with irritating ringtones, and CCTV cameras in bigfoot culture.

Once integrated into domestic life, the average bigfoot seems to take particular pleasure in trips to the cinema. They have been observed sneaking in (usually without a ticket as they don't seem to be able to grasp the concept of capitalism), and have been known to stay for up to three or four days at a time.

(See also Yeti, Yowie, Agogwe, Skunk Ape, Orang Pendek, Almas and some Benefits Agency staff.)

EATS	Nuts, berries, leaves. Cheese and cucumber sandwiches (but only with the crusts cut off).
LIKES	Peace and quiet. Walking in the rain. Films (pretty much anything with Sigourney Weaver in).
DISLIKES	Campers. Anyone with a camera. Overzealous cinema ticket staff.

ELMENDORF BEAST

Often thought to be nothing more than a coyote with mange, in fact this so-called 'beast' is lovable, extremely loyal, and an absolute whizz round the local dog agility courses.

UNICORN

Unicorns are a fabulous idea for a pet, particularly if you have children. The gentler ones will love to ride them, and the more adventurous will have hours of fun swinging from the horn, or attempting to impale their friends on it when Mummy isn't looking. They are, however, notoriously difficult to handle.

It is well known that a unicorn can only be tamed by a virgin, and preferably a female one. So…while you have a young daughter in the house you should be fine, but once she grows up and moves out or, Heaven forbid, goes off to camp with her Brownie pack for a week, you are, I'm afraid, in lumber.

Dead lumber.

This is when you will discover just how difficult it can be to entertain your adult friends at a posh cocktail party. The first you will know of trouble is when you notice, out of the corner of your eye, a curious-looking horn poking round the door frame.

The next thing, your family unicorn will be slurping punch out of your crystal cut-glass punchbowl that you haven't dared use since before the children were born, and munching his way through the *hors d'oeuvres*. This is roughly the point at which you will discover that unicorns are, in fact, herd animals, and he will have a dozen or so of his friends waiting at the door to come and join the party.

YETI

MOST CRYPTOZOOLOGICAL ANIMALS ARE, BY THEIR VERY NATURE, UNKNOWN OR HIDDEN, AND THAT TENDS TO MEAN THEY DON'T GET A GREAT DEAL OF PUBLICITY.

It's not often that you see headlines like 'Drowning woman saved by Mongolian death worm', and the celebrity gossip pages rarely feature candid shots of 'Florida skunk ape caught in compromising position with chambermaid'. But let's face it, everyone and his dog (or Mongolian death worm, as the case may be) has heard of the yeti.

Some people prefer to think of it as a particular type of snowman, while others stick with 'yeti' because, let's face it, abonima… anobinmal…abdominal snowman is so damned difficult to spell, and it's even harder to say, especially after you've had a drink or two and spent a few hours regaling your friends with amusing anecdotes about that time you took your pet to the local church fundraiser and he tried to drag the vicar's wife off to some obscure hideout in the mountains.

This is a common behavioural problem with yetis as a species, and even if you don't actually live near any mountain ranges, they seem unable to break the habit of dragging random people off to the perceived safety of a mountain cave (or local car wash if that is all they can find) and nursing them back to health before vanishing as mysteriously as they appeared.

This is a purely instinctive behaviour and their compassion is really a very endearing quality...although at times it can be quite annoying if you were actually just trying to buy a loaf of bread in the local supermarket and weren't in any serious danger of falling into a coma from a combination of exhaustion and freezing conditions, and actually would really just like to be left alone to go home and make a peanut butter sandwich, thank you so *very* much.

And in any case, they're not abominable at all, they're really rather sweet. The ~~aboni~~...~~anomi~~...yeti must be one of the best known of all the cryptids, and as such, is often the creature of choice for the new cryptid owner. They do require a cool environment, however, and it is really not sufficient to simply let them sleep in the fridge.

With the global warming issue, the yeti's native habitat is being eroded to such an extent that it is now an endangered species. As such, it is suggested that if you do choose to home a yeti you ensure you take on a breeding pair.

If you are successful and your home is blessed with the pitter-patter of 600lb feet scampering about, you will find that the young yeti is a playful animal. Favourite games include hide and seek, and Twister.

The yeti themselves are fully aware of their status as endangered, and realise that exposure to the wrong kind of person could result in some very unpleasant tests. As such, they are quite happy to lie down and pretend to be a furry rug if you should have unexpected visitors.

DRAGON

SO WELL KNOWN IN BOTH EASTERN AND WESTERN CULTURE, THIS HARDLY QUALIFIES AS A CRYPTOZOOLOGICAL CREATURE AT ALL.

However, the authorities, in their wisdom, still refuse to recognise it as real, so for the moment at least, you don't require a licence to own one.

If you decide to opt for one of the fire-breathing breeds, however, do please bear in mind the proximity of your house to farmland, bales of hay, that sort of thing.

If you own a dragon it is almost impossible to obtain insurance against fire, or indeed against sword-wielding, acne-covered youths in armour – and these will turn up on your doorstep with alarming regularity.

EATS	Damsels...No, sorry, that should be damsons (the fruit). Seriously, they don't eat people, goodness only knows where this idea came from. They much prefer pizza, and sometimes a few chillies.
LIKES	Virgins. Bales of hay.
DISLIKES	Men with swords.

WAHEELA

THERE IS A TREND AMONG A CERTAIN SEGMENT OF THE POPULATION TOWARDS OWNING SMALL DOGS THAT CAN BE ADORNED WITH PINK RIBBONS AND EASILY TRANSPORTED IN A DESIGNER HANDBAG.

If you are one of these people, then you will probably not be drawn to the waheela. This large, wolf-like animal stands about 4ft high at the shoulder, and is not known for its ability to fit into a Louis Vuitton.

Very little else is known of this rare species, and there are no known captive specimens. It is believed that there are small populations of these animals living in remote areas of Canada, but they do not take kindly to uninvited visitors, so do tread carefully if this is your chosen pet.

The waheela is a magnificent beast with long, white fur (making it absolutely perfect for those who like to snuggle in front of the fire with a cup of hot chocolate and a good book).

The few cryptozoologists who have managed to study this animal report that it is more stockily built than an average wolf, and has large paws relative to its body size.

Anyone who knows anything about dogs will know that large paws mean only one thing – this is a *puppy*, so goodness only knows how big it will be when fully grown. If you really are set on one of these you will need a larger than average dog kennel.

GREMLINS

These are social animals, living in tribal groups. No reliably accurate description exists, although in popular culture they have come to be known as small creatures with pointed ears and evil grins. This is almost certainly NOT what gremlins actually look like.

Known for sabotaging items such as aircraft, motor-cycles, computers and the like, these animals are the scourge of modern society. It is their insatiable curiosity, rather than any actual malevolence, which drives them to deconstruct just about any mechanical object they can get their claws on.

Frankly, if you are on the receiving end of their activities, it doesn't matter how much of it is down to idle curiosity and how much is down to mischief, the end result is the same – absolute and utter chaos.

As a general rule, they are best avoided. Seriously. Don't go near them. I'm not kidding.

TATZELWURM

HERE WE HAVE CAUGHT AN ANIMAL RIGHT IN THE ACT OF EVOLVING. THIS 6FT-LONG SERPENT FOUND IN AREAS OF THE SWISS ALPS, AUSTRIA AND FRANCE HAS FRONT LEGS, BUT NO HIND LEGS.

It also has a face with a decidedly feline, rather than reptilian, appearance. It is largely aquatic but is known to live in caves.

Evolutionarily speaking, it has not yet been established if this is a cat that moved into the water because it was easier to catch fish that way, or a serpent that dragged itself onto land in the desperate pursuit of something to eat *other than fish*. Either way, it has clearly not quite finished with the evolution business, and really needs to make up its mind what it wants to be.

If you choose to home one, you will have to quickly ascertain at which end of the cat vs serpent scale your particular pet dwells, and look after it accordingly.

If it is more of a feline persuasion, you may as well forget about having a garden pond with fish as they won't last more than about five minutes. If it is more serpent-like, you will need a bloody big fish tank, and none of that fake sunken treasure rubbish, it will want *real* sunken treasure, and something more challenging in the way of entertainment. You could try sudoku.

Generally lovable and happy to be cuddled, but if you should get on the wrong side of your tatzelwurm you will quickly find out that it can spray you with a rather unpleasant toxin. Most A&E departments are not familiar with the tatzelwurm so if you try to explain what has happened, and stick rigidly to your story even when they try to persuade you it was nothing more than skunk spray, do not be surprised if you find yourself in a straitjacket, getting carted off somewhere for psychiatric evaluation.

SELMA

Here we look at the options for importing lake monsters, such as the Norwegian Selma and the Swedish Storsjoodjuret. As has been said before, the use of the term 'monster' is wholly inappropriate. The worst you are likely to get is a small nip if you do not let go of the fish quickly enough.

These magnificent creatures make a joyous addition to any aquarium, and with the right care and attention they can be as awe-inspiring a sight as any dolphin.

They make brilliant pets as, much like their close relative, Nessie, they are very gentle animals, possessed of a calm and serene nature.

You may, however, encounter problems if you try to keep these animals indoors. They tend to drip algae all over the furniture, and are not generally considered easy to house-train.

HELLHOUND

CONSIDER THE HELLHOUND. LAPDOG TO THE RICH AND FAMOUS, OR DEMONIC HOUND STRAIGHT FROM THE FIRES OF HELL?

These animals are large, frighteningly strong and terrifyingly fast, with piercing, glowing eyes. They are believed to guard the gateway to Hell, but in fact many find useful employment at the local scrapyard.

Coming face-to-face with one of these creatures is an overwhelmingly scary experience. They tend to growl menacingly for no apparent reason, and give the distinct impression that tearing people limb from limb is their absolute favourite pastime – which is odd really because actually your average hellhound loves nothing more than having its tummy tickled.

EBU GOGO

The Ebu Gogo is a socially challenged 'hobbit'-type creature, not quite as adventurous as his cousin, Disco a Gogo (a real party animal). This somewhat geek-like creature is rather more interested in science fiction than parties. He is short, reaching only about 3ft in height when fully grown, and has a pot-belly and sticky-out ears.

All in all, quite a looker, and very popular with the ladies.

The image shows text on the book: "WAR OF THE WORLDS"

CRYPTIDS FOR PECUNIARY ENHANCEMENT

THERE IS A REMOTE POSSIBILITY
YOU MAY MAKE A FEW QUID FROM YOUR
PET HERE AND THERE...BUT DON'T ORDER
THE PRIVATE JET JUST YET.

GNOMES

HERE, WE ASK IF THE 'INNOCENT' GARDEN GNOME IS REALLY AS HARMLESS AS IT WOULD HAVE US BELIEVE, OR IS IT IN FACT FURTIVELY PLOTTING AGAINST THE HUMAN RACE – AND IF SO, WHAT PRECAUTIONS SHOULD YOU TAKE TO AVERT DISASTER, ANNIHILATION, AND GENERAL INCONVENIENCE?

Gnomes, as is well known, are small humanoid creatures with beards and pointy hats. They live close to the earth (probably because they are not tall enough to get any farther away from it), and care for nature and animals. Some people like to have gnome ornaments in their gardens in the belief that they will help out with the gardening at night. There is, however, little evidence to support this theory, and many thinkers are coming to believe that the gnomes are actually 'lazy buggers', preferring to spend their time fishing, sleeping or smoking pipes rather than doing any actual work.

Garden gnomes may appear to be made from clay or resin. Do not be fooled – this is merely their dormant state.

Gnomes traditionally go to great lengths to perpetuate the myth that they are inanimate, often maintaining the same 'fishing', 'sleeping' or 'smoking a pipe' pose for months at a time. When they do choose to move they are generally very careful to ensure no one is watching, although full-action moving gnomes have recently been sighted in Argentina.

This development has caused some concern among gnome aficionados as it represents an escalation in the unspoken war of wills, and some have posited that it may be an early indication of things to come. Perhaps they are already preparing for the gnome apocalypse and taking steps towards what is believed to be their primary goal – total world domination.

It might be a good idea to invest in one of those old Cold War-era bomb shelters. Just in case.

EATS	No one knows. If your garden has gnomes, however, you will probably find a distinct absence of ostriches in the vicinity. Read into that what you will.
LIKES	Fishing. Sleeping. Smoking pipes. Plotting world domination.
DISLIKES	Being expected to do any actual work in the garden.

TERATORN

MANY PEOPLE, QUITE ERRONEOUSLY, BELIEVE THAT THE TERATORN IS AN EXTINCT BIRD THAT DIED OUT IN THE PLEISTOCENE EPOCH.

Those in the know, however, are not falling for that one. After all, that's what they told us about the coelacanth, and look how that turned out.

Much like the dodo, the teratorn is, in fact, merely incognito, having retired from public life some time ago.

Homing one of these is a huge commitment. You can't just think of it as an oversized budgie, and stick it in a cage with a little mirror for entertainment.

These are large birds, with a wingspan of over 12ft (and some as large as 25ft), and frankly, they don't fit easily into cages, and even if they did, they wouldn't be best pleased about it. They are magnificent, regal creatures which really need to be given the freedom to fly.

Rest assured, however, teratorns are loyal and loving, and will always return to you if you look after them properly.

Because of their large size, it can prove a bit difficult to hide them, and it is advised that you don't let them out over populated areas, or people will see them and then the next thing you know there will be all kinds of problems. If the hunting, shooting and fishing brigade get wind of this there's no telling how long the species will last. They are gentle creatures, and really quite trusting in nature. It is our duty to protect them.

It is primarily for this reason that conservationists propagate the myth that the species is, in fact, extinct. Indeed, there are no teratorns left in the wild and if you wish to source one you will need to go through an authorised breeder, and this will involve quite stringent security and suitability checks. If you've ever had so much as a parking ticket you may as well forget it. They don't hand these eggs over to just anyone, you know.

In recent years there has been a rise in popularity of the homing teratorn as a pet. For some decades now, there has been an open competition, with fiercely contested timed races staged by wild-eyed owners, each desperate to prove that their teratorn is the ultimate racing teratorn.

Back in the 1940s, a few of these homing teratorns were spotted by members of the public over Illinois and Missouri. It was a terrible breach of protocol, but in fairness it was a more innocent time and the owners involved were more guilty of being a bit naive than actually malicious. Since then, security has been much tighter, and the races are usually conducted at night over unpopulated areas.

ROPEN

The ropen is a flying pterosaur-like bird from Papua New Guinea. Somewhat similar to the kongamato, but with the added feature of bioluminescence when it flies.

This could be an ideal pet for those wishing to save on the lighting bills during the long winter months.

SNALLYGASTER

IS THE SNALLYGASTER BEST KEPT FOR GUARD DUTIES OR EGG PRODUCTION? GIVEN THAT THE EGGS HAVE AN INCUBATION PERIOD THAT RUNS INTO DECADES THIS IS VERY MUCH A VENTURE FOR THE FAR-SIGHTED ENTREPRENEUR.

The snallygaster is exceptionally rare, and it is believed there are only a handful of breeding pairs left in the wild. This is very much the cryptozoological equivalent of the duck-billed platypus, in that it seems to be a little bit of everything. It's basically a large flying reptile with a beak and teeth. So far not so very different to the kongamato, but here's where it gets a bit wacky – it also has one large eye and octopus-like tentacles.

Although it is said to carry off humans and drink their blood, in fact, it is a peaceable animal, actually quite shy and retiring. It is not known how it came to have such a bad reputation.

Anyone carried off by this animal has surely misunderstood its intentions. Members of the active campaign group, SOS (Save Our Snallygasters) are certain the animal is merely looking for companionship, and exsanguination is only ever done in fun. Seriously, some people just can't take a joke.

Some sources report that the snallygaster is believed to have a phobia of the number seven, and further state that nervous householders often place a seven-pointed star on their buildings in a curious attempt to scare the animal away.

It has not yet been determined what evolutionary advantage this supposed fear of the number seven confers on the snallygaster, but in any case the seven-pointed stars have little practical effect. While they are, for the most part, a decorative addition to any dwelling, the truth is the snallygaster can't actually count.

MONGOLIAN DEATH WORM

Really good for the soil in your garden. Just be careful where you put your spade, because this lot can fight back.

ELVES

NOT A FAMOUS ROCK SINGER. ELVES, AS IS NOW WELL KNOWN, FORM THE LARGER PART OF SANTA'S WORKFORCE, AND ASIDE FROM SOME UNION PROBLEMS A FEW YEARS AGO, THEY ARE ON THE WHOLE A VERY HAPPY BUNCH.

If you want to home one of these, however, you must be prepared to supply an infinite amount of milk and cookies.

Indeed, an adequate supply of such refreshments is a legally binding requirement of any owner and is enshrined in the employment contract.

Once upon a time, elves (of pretty much any persuasion) were a lovable, easy-going bunch. They were known for sneaking into houses at night to tidy up for overworked mums, or cobble shoes for elderly shoemakers, never asking for thanks or expecting any kind of reward. All that changed with unionisation and nowadays the elves are extremely clear on what does, and perhaps more significantly what does *not*, form part of their duties.

For example, they will not fetch a ball, they will not chase mice, and they will most definitely not have any truck with tummy-tickling, which is considered degrading to elves, and could in fact lead to strike action.

Their philosophy is basically this: leave the bouncing around, playing with balls of string and the like to the more traditional pets, and let us get on with the serious business of being an elf. They do, in fact, make excellent working pets as long as you respect them as equals, and don't expect them to curl up at the foot of your bed. They will want their own private room with en suite, and furthermore they demand quite a generous pension.

Tread carefully with this one. Some cryptids may eat you, but this lot are not afraid of litigation and will hit you where it really hurts – your wallet.

FEAR LIATH MOR

Also known as the Big Grey Man, this is basically
Scotland's answer to Bigfoot, although this variety is taller
and even more hairy than your average sasquatch.

Living predominantly in the Cairngorm mountains, the
animal is rumoured to have paranormal powers. While
these animals could productively be put to work in the
fields of tea-leaf reading and seances, in the wild their
talents tend to be used only for such mundane things as
controlling the fog, which they do purely for the pretty
effect it has on the mountaintops.

Unfortunately, the sight of one of these large bipedal
primates, often glimpsed only through gaps in the fog,
tends to create panic in hill-walkers, who then inexplicably
run away and jump off cliffs to escape.

As a result, poor old fear liath mor has developed a bit
of a complex and is starting to think people don't really
like him.

Particularly stylish and debonair among the bipedal
primates, this one is sometimes seen wearing a top hat and
drinking Scotch whisky. If you are a flat-cap sort of person,
then perhaps this isn't the pet for you.

You may wish to look into bulk discounts, which may
be obtained at the local tuxedo hire shop, and consider
what remedial action to take if your pet keeps leaping tall
buildings and jumping out of helicopters to leave boxes of
chocolates in strange womens' bedrooms.

FUR-BEARING TROUT

Widely believed to be a hoax, but in fact this is an interesting choice for the more enterprising cryptid owner.
  This creature offers two ways to make money from your pet – the food trade and the fur trade. Not to mention the Best of Breed competitions in which big-money prizes are awarded in fiercely fought competitions for the most colourful coat and the snuggliest fur.

TROLL

THERE IS SOME DEBATE AS TO WHETHER THE TROLL CAN BE TRULY CLASSED AS A CRYPTOZOOLOGICAL CREATURE SINCE A NUMBER OF THEM HAVE ACTUALLY INTEGRATED QUITE WELL INTO WESTERN SOCIETY, AND CAN BE FOUND WORKING IN MANY LOCAL GOVERNMENT OFFICES.

It is fair to assume that they have been corrupted by exposure to unnatural levels of bureaucracy, because the officious behaviour displayed by those trolls living in cities is markedly different to those in their natural environment – the mountainous regions of Scandinavia. Here, they are a gentle and peaceable species, unfairly pilloried by so-called civilised society, accused of lurking under bridges waiting to eat people, when in fact they had simply stopped for a rest and had no intention whatsoever of snacking on anything, human or otherwise.

The very name 'troll' has an unfortunate association with people who post unpleasant comments on the interweb. In fact, trolls are not very computer-literate and many of them still use an old Atari for their computer gaming needs, finding Pong a particularly sophisticated and challenging game.

CRYPTIDS FOR THE MILDLY RECKLESS

WITH A GLINT IN THE EYE AND
A RELAXED APPROACH TO HEALTH
AND SAFETY REGULATIONS.

MERMAID

OK, popular culture has this one down as a glamorous young woman with a pleasing attitude and a fish tail. Don't let them kid you. If you have ever lived with teenagers, you will know how frustrating it can be waiting for them to come out of the bathroom. Imagine how much worse it will be when your pet *literally* lives in the bath.

Add to the mix the fact that mermaids are extremely vain and can happily spend entire days just looking at themselves in the mirror and brushing their hair.

Then there's the mood swings. Mermaids live in a perpetual state of adolescence (face it, have you ever seen an elderly mermaid pushing along a Zimmer frame?) so you get all the teenage angst, the tantrums over spots, refusing to tidy their rooms, obsessing over musicians (generally Country Joe and the Fish or Hootie and the Blowfish), and generally just looking at you like you have no right still being on the planet at your greatly advanced age (as with most teenagers, this means anything over 30).

Frankly, if you have a teenage daughter you really don't need a mermaid. If you don't have a teenage daughter, just invite one of your friends' teenage daughters to stay the weekend and after that you won't even *want* a mermaid any more.

PHOENIX

AAH, THE PHOENIX…EVERYONE LOVES THE PHOENIX.
IT HAS BECOME A SYMBOL OF HOPE AND OPTIMISM THE
WORLD OVER.

Sporting vibrant golden yellow and red plumage, this is really quite a beautiful bird…but the problem is, it *knows* it's beautiful. As a result, it's just a little too big for its boots. In fact, it's an arrogant little so-and-so, according to some experts.

Also known as the firebird, it is supposed by many that the phoenix lives a solitary life because it is enigmatic and mysterious. In fact, it lives a solitary life because no one likes a smartarse. These birds are vain, selfish and self-important. Any phoenix owner will tell you it's not so much enigmatic as it is a 'bloody pain in the neck' (to quote the breeders' handbook).

A brief glance at any decent manual on bird care will tell you that birds enjoy playing with toys, especially wooden toys, as they have some bizarre, innate need to destroy wood. This is done, apparently, to show off to other birds, and also just for the sheer fun of it.

This sort of behaviour is probably manageable when you are dealing with a budgie and a small toy made of twisted cardboard... but scale this up to the phoenix and we are talking mass destruction of your dining-room table and any other wooden fixtures and fittings.

Many phoenix owners have simply given up repairing window and door frames and just accept that the draughts are the price they pay for owning such a rare and exclusive breed.

Folklore has it that as it nears the end of its life the phoenix will build a nest of cinnamon twigs, which it then ignites. It is not known if this is achieved by the use of proprietary fire-lighters, or by rubbing two sticks together. Either way, it makes a heck of a mess of the carpet. And take it from me, the insurance company won't want to know. You try mentioning 'fire damage' and 'pet phoenix' in the same sentence and just see how quickly they hang up.

In fact, this business of setting fire to things isn't just an end-of-life ritual, it can be a daily occurrence. The animal has an extremely unstable metabolism and the slightest little thing can upset the delicate chemical balance, causing random sparks to fly up from its body and spontaneously combust, leaving a trail of little fires around your house.

While this may have been very pretty when the phoenix was first domesticated, and cave-dwelling humans were actually quite pleased about the heat and light given off by these little fires, the brutal truth is it really doesn't work so well in a suburban semi.

ALMAS

ANOTHER EXAMPLE OF A NEANDERTHAL-LIKE APEMAN.

There are many variations on this theme, and it's really just a question of finding the one which best suits your own lifestyle.

The almas is found in the mountainous regions of Mongolia and central Asia, and is known to be extremely strong – a perfect combination if you live at the top of a hill and need help carrying the shopping home.

The mature almas will usually reach only around 5ft in height, so should present no great problems to those in more compact accommodation.

Although extremely cute as a baby, the fully-grown almas is widely considered to lose much of its appeal to all but the truly dedicated owner. They have quite prominent eyebrow ridges, and when combined with the protruding jaw and receding chin, this gives them a very specific appearance which some have compared to the Neanderthal, or indeed, the counter staff in certain fast-food chains.

They live on a simple diet of foliage and grass, and can be as good as any sheep for keeping the lawn neatly trimmed.

Don't expect this breed to actually do any work around the house, however. Their love of all things horticultural may conjure up images of hard-working, lusty gardeners with calloused hands and rippling biceps…but the truth is somewhat less exciting, and significantly more hairy.

They will keep the lawn trimmed as long as it suits them to do so, but won't work to a set timetable. They will pick flowers if you ask them to, but are more than likely to have eaten them before you have managed to extricate the vase from its hiding place under the sink.

In short, this is not the most obliging of breeds and cannot always be relied upon to return your devotion. Indeed, the almas has a well-known attitude problem and any simple request ('Please pass the salt', for example), is just as likely to result in you being beaten senseless with a bunch of half-eaten daffodil stems as anything else.

The almas is totally self-centred and will alternately ignore you or grunt at you, depending on…well actually no one has yet figured out what it depends on. Best to keep out of their way as much as possible in fact. Consider homing an almas as a similar commitment to homing the average human adolescent. Moody, hormonal, lazy and sullen. This is a laugh-a-minute choice.

EATS	Grass, leaves, flowers. Be careful what you stock your garden with, as they won't distinguish between harmless daisies and daffodils, and the potentially dangerous plants such as foxglove. They are also quite partial to next-door's prize gardenias.
LIKES	Houseplants. Garden plants. Pictures of plants.
DISLIKES	Lawnmowers.

CENTAUR

HALF-MAN, HALF-HORSE, WHAT MORE COULD A WOMAN ASK FOR IN A BLIND DATE?

Actually, these animals tend to have a bit of an attitude problem and, to be fair, do not make the best household pets. They trail muddy hoofprints all over your new beige carpet and get ever so uppity about people who don't slow down for horses...or people who *do* slow down...or in fact just people in general.

Psychologists call it inter-species confusion and warn of the dangers of aggravating them by drawing attention to the fact they are...well, to put it bluntly, neither one thing nor the other.

Basically they have the most gigantic chip on their shoulder, and to be fair it must be pretty irritating when you're trying to buy new shoes and they only come in pairs so you have to fork out double what a 'normal' person has to pay. And all the park benches are designed for humans, and the cars, and the bicycles...and as for claiming benefits, well the counter staff just snigger into their coffee cups.

All in all, perhaps we really shouldn't be surprised that centaurs seem to be in a permanent bad mood.

None of the experts have yet come up with a workable solution.

Best to just avoid them if you can and stick to sea monsters – at least you know where you are with a sea monster. It might eat you, but at least you don't have to listen to it moaning and complaining about it first.

EATS	Whatever it wants. Quite partial to hay…but only if it thinks no one is watching.
LIKES	No one has yet managed to answer this one.
DISLIKES	People. Gymkhanas. Horse racing. Pony trekking. In fact, anything where creatures of the equine persuasion might be considered to be subject to exploitation of *any* kind. Glue factories – they especially hate glue factories.

GOBLINS

They're short. They're mischievous. They're generally bad-tempered, and love to play tricks such as spilling milk or hiding things. Pretty much the same as living with the average human toddler. Nothing new or mysterious about this one.

GIANT ANACONDA

THERE IS LITTLE DISPUTE ABOUT THE EXISTENCE OF ANACONDAS, SO REALLY THE ONLY KUDOS TO BE GAINED HERE IS FROM OWNING A PARTICULARLY LARGE ONE.

Normal anacondas, the ones scientists are quite happy to accept are real, usually grow to around 20–30ft in length, but the giant anaconda (*Sucuriju gigante*) is reported as growing anywhere from 80–130ft long.

Serious problems persist for those attempting to import these creatures from their native South America, as let's face it, who has a suitcase big enough to hide one of these under the holiday souvenirs? And do you *really* fancy explaining that oversized wriggling snakeskin 'handbag' to the Customs official?

You should be aware that furtive-looking travellers arriving from this part of the world do tend to come under a little more scrutiny than your average duty-free-toting tourist.

Nevertheless, if you feel this is the pet for you, and the prospect of jail-time for illegal importation of a dangerous animal is not a concern, it is worth remembering that quarantine procedures do not apply to those animals not recognised as real by the mainstream scientific community.

So there's really very little point in even mentioning it as you walk through the airport security gate, dragging your bulging suitcase. To be honest, you wouldn't be doing them any favours by announcing the fact that you are surreptitiously attempting to import a hissing, spitting killing machine into the country, anyway.

After all, if you tell them about it, they *have* to search your case, and once you open the case all kinds of reptilian hell will break loose. What may start as an affectionate cuddle as the anaconda wraps itself around the official, will soon turn into a death grip and – as we all know – being crushed or suffocated to death may cause offence.

Assuming you do manage to smuggle it through Customs you will find it a loving and affectionate pet…at least, it will try to cuddle you at every opportunity, so – putting the best spin possible on the situation – we must assume that this is merely an attempt at bonding, rather than food preparation.

EATS	Bulls, people, whole pineapples, Customs officials, whatever the hell it pleases, really.
LIKES	Hide and seek…well, hide and *pounce*, anyway.
DISLIKES	Bicycles – it's too hard to work the pedals without feet.

HOOP SNAKE

A rather bizarre reptile which is often mistaken for a
perfectly ordinary snake, and for this reason its existence
has not been accepted by modern science.

The curious feature of this snake is its ability to grab its
tail in its mouth, forming a hoop shape (hence the rather
unimaginative name), and then roll along the ground after
its prey, thereby achieving far greater speeds than would be
attained using normal snake-slithering methods.

The snake then, at the last minute, uncoils itself and
lashes out with its venomous tail, striking the victim…
unless said victim has the presence of mind to hide behind
any conveniently situated trees, in which case the tree takes
the hit, and the snake lies trembling and twitching from
the impact, allowing the 'victim' to escape, laughing, into
the night.

Owning one of these could bring new and exciting
dimensions to hula-hooping.

OLD YELLOW TOP

Old Yellow Top is pretty much your ordinary everyday bipedal primate – except for its apparent propensity for the use of hair dye. As the name suggests, this animal seems to prefer conventional shades such as 'Ash Blonde', or 'Island Sunrise'.

There is much debate among owners about whether it is wise to try to expand its horizons to include shades such as 'Sunset Over the Sewage Works' or even something a little more adventurous like 'Cotton-candy Surprise with Sky-blue Highlights'.

There is no consensus of opinion as yet, but if you do decide to give this a try, please make sure you have fully researched any local rehabilitation and recovery centres for your treatment should you inadvertently allow Old Yellow Top to get hold of a mirror and see what you have done.

BERGMAN'S BEAR

THIS ONE IS BASICALLY A REALLY LARGE BEAR. WHEN I SAY LARGE, I MEAN *HUGE*… AND WHEN I SAY BEAR, I MEAN THE MOST ADORABLE, HUGGLY, GREAT BIG TEDDY BEAR YOU CAN IMAGINE.

It was identified in the early 1900s based on the evidence of a skin and a few footprints. Sounds reasonable enough to me.

Like so many other cryptids, its existence had been known to the locals for quite some time but, of course, that didn't count. In fact, even now it isn't accepted by the scientific community since no corpse has ever been found, only a skin. They do like to get their hands on a dead body before they are prepared to accept that something is actually real.

The general consensus of scientific opinion seems to be that if this is a real animal then it's extinct. So, again, it doesn't count – at least to the scientists.

And yet other branches of science are perfectly prepared to talk seriously about things like black holes as if there is absolutely no question about their existence; when in truth black holes remain to this day, an unproven theory, and no one has ever found a black hole corpse to dissect (indeed, no one has even made a plaster cast of its footprints).

Bergman's bear, also known as the God Bear due to its enormous size, is found in the Kamchatka region of Russia. Actually, it would probably be more accurate to say that it *isn't* found there, but of all the places in the world where it isn't found, this is the most likely place to not find it.

The region is known to support enormous brown bears, but Bergman's bear is large, even by those standards. It has a coat of short black hair, and humungous giant feet ('humungous' being the technical term, naturally). At least…it leaves humungous giant footprints wherever it goes, a fact which has led some to posit that perhaps it just wears humungous giant clown shoes to trick the scientific community into thinking it has big feet, and therefore deserves its own separate classification.

If you are fortunate enough to get one of your own, you will find that it requires quite a large garden for exercise, and it's generally considered best to have some sort of outdoor kennel for it to live in. Naturally you don't want something with such humungous giant feet trailing mud in all over your nice clean carpet.

Rumour has it that there are still a few of them around, hidden deep in the more remote areas of Russia, and it is just possible to find a specimen turning up occasionally on eBay, so it's worth taking a look every now and again.

EATS	Primarily fish. Also they do enjoy quite a varied diet of roots, nuts, berries and the occasional jar of honey.
LIKES	People. But it probably couldn't eat a whole one.
DISLIKES	People who queue in the basket aisle with more than ten items.

FOUKE MONSTER

Imaginatively named for the town in Arkansas where it has been sighted most frequently, but also known as the Jonesville Monster and the Boggy Creek Monster. It can get terribly confusing when you are trying to tell the authorities exactly which monster it was that attacked you in the woods.

In fact, this animal is quite mild-mannered and not generally given to random attacks. Admittedly, it isn't *too* difficult to see why misguided locals have coined the term 'monster', following a number of reported 'attacks' on both people and homes. But in truth the poor thing is merely misunderstood and, seriously, people need to get a grip and try to see things from the other person's point of view before they start complaining about being chased and beaten. Can't take a joke? Well, don't go wandering around the woods at night then.

Unlike most primates, this is a nocturnal animal and, given the amount of noise generated by human populations during the day, it's easy to understand why the Fouke monster might crawl out of its den after a disturbed and restless day trying to get some shut-eye, and go off in search of the inconsiderate jerks who kept it awake. Who among us has *not* felt the urge to wrap a tree around someone's head after a disturbed day without sleep?

CRYPTIDS FOR THE SHEER UNADULTERATED JOY OF IT

ENTIRELY AT YOUR OWN RISK, OF COURSE.

NESSIE

SO, HERE'S THE THING. WE ALL KNOW ABOUT NESSIE, RIGHT? IT'S A SORT OF OPEN SECRET IN SCOTLAND.

The locals will smile and wink as they wish you luck in your search, giving every impression that they think you are a complete fool and you have no hope whatsoever of finding a plesiosaur in Loch Ness because, after all, there's no such thing.

The truth is, they are ever so slightly worried that one day someone will take a nice clear picture of Nessie and then the tranquility of this beautiful part of the world will be forever destroyed as an unending stream of tourists, media and scientists flock to the area. It's busy enough without any proof of the 'monster' – can you imagine what it would be like once everyone *knew* it was there? In fact, this animal is part of a fragile ecosystem, and the primary concern of the conservationists is the protection of the species.

For this reason, a small but dedicated band of Nessie protectors work tirelessly to maintain the status quo, and take whatever steps are deemed necessary to perpetuate the illusion that the Loch Ness Monster is just a misidentified lump of wood, or a seal, or a dolphin. They toil relentlessly on a carefully crafted plan to make the public think it's all a hoax, or perhaps even a sturgeon that just got a bit lost.

Now, this isn't as simple a task as you might think. There was, after all, that infamous photo of a serpent's head sticking out of the water, which hit the papers back in the 1930s. In fairness, the photo *did* adhere to the strict guidelines now required by conservationists: it was grainy and not too clear, and there was nothing else in the photo to give a sense of scale or distance. Nevertheless, the photo did convince a good percentage of the population that Nessie was real, and many people dutifully set out to find the animal.

There was, for a time, a real danger that someone would actually go and prove the existence of Nessie beyond all doubt, and that was the last thing the conservationists wanted. It was becoming such a problem that, frankly, something drastic had to be done. So, in a carefully orchestrated campaign, they managed to put about the story that what the photo *actually* showed was merely a small toy mocked up to look like a sea monster, and it was all just a big practical joke.

This cover story seems to have been widely accepted, and has pretty much restored the status quo. Now people can go back to thinking it's all a hoax, and Nessie can get on with the serious business of frolicking in the loch, undisturbed by hordes of scalpel-wielding scientists bent on taking DNA samples.

It's a well-guarded secret, even among cryptozoologists, that there are a handful of captive Nessies living as much-loved pets in homes across Great Britain. Should you be fortunate enough to obtain one you will be required to sign official secrecy papers to guarantee that you will never release any clear, non-grainy photographs, or anything else that might be considered definitive evidence of the existence of this animal.

QUEENSLAND TIGER

There is much debate about whether the Queensland Tiger is a real animal or perhaps an extinct one that people merely *think* is real, based on the notoriously unreliable evidence of actually having seen it.

Another controversial issue surrounding this animal is its classification. Is it, as the name suggests, a member of the cat family or, as some experts maintain, a marsupial?

Well, there is one easy way to find out…once you have got yours home you might like to try tickling its tummy to see if there is a pouch there, a sure-fire indicator that it is a marsupial. Alternatively you may find that having your hand ripped to shreds for attempting such an intimate examination proves irrefutably that it is a kitty cat.

PERUVIAN MYSTERY JAGUAR

What, you may ask, actually *is* the mystery behind the Peruvian mystery jaguar, and can you, in fact, source a Peruvian mystery jaguar in Peru?

Well, according to recent research it kind of looks like the only real mystery is in regard to the pigmentation and markings of the animal's coat...so I guess it's really just a fashion issue.

Fashion, as is well known, is an important aspect of cryptozoology. It is *vitally* important that you wear the correct attire if you are out in the wilds in search of the unknown. Stiletto heels simply won't do.

Likewise, it is important for the *unknown* to be appropriately clothed. This animal does prefer the designs of one or two very exclusive fashion houses, and will swap from one fur coat to another according to the latest issue of *Vogue*, or sometimes simply for the sheer fun of it.

GIANT

Take my tip, stick with something that is easier to look after, like a great white shark or perhaps an angry crocodile.

This one doesn't really have a lot going for it as a pet. It isn't cute, it isn't cuddly, it isn't even particularly smart. It does, however, like to stomp about the place shouting silly threats about eating people. Oh, and it isn't even bright enough to duck when going through doors so you will find all your door frames end up with big, messy-looking holes at the top.

EMELA-NTOUKA

THIS POOR CREATURE SEEMS TO HAVE BEEN COBBLED TOGETHER FROM THE SPARE PARTS OF OTHER ANIMALS, ANOTHER CRYPTOZOOLOGICAL FORAY INTO THE DESIGN HOUSE WHICH BROUGHT US THE DUCK-BILLED PLATYPUS.

It has the body of a rhinoceros, the tail of a crocodile and, just for good measure, a humungous giant horn on its snout.

It is often described as 'irritable' but a more appropriate term would probably be 'bloody furious'. Many experts believe this can be attributed to the common belief that emela-ntouka horn is a powerful aphrodisiac. Sadly, it hasn't done much for the emela-ntouka as it is now an endangered species due to excessive poaching.

EATS	Mostly grass, but given half a chance they will polish off a bowl of chocolate-flavoured breakfast cereal before you can say, 'sugar rush'.
LIKES	Peace and quiet. Neil Diamond.
DISLIKES	People who spread bloody stupid rumours about emela-ntouka horn being an aphrodisiac, and – even more – people who *believe* bloody stupid rumours that emela-ntouka horn is an aphrodisiac.

KONGAMATO

THERE IS SOME DISPUTE AS TO THE CLASSIFICATION OF THIS MAGNIFICENT BEAST. SOME SCHOLARS MAINTAIN IT IS A BAT, WHILE OTHERS ARE CONVINCED IT IS A BIRD.

In fact, it is more accurately described as a pterosaur.

Conventional science states that the pterosaurs died out some time ago, along with the vast majority of other dinosaurs…but that's *exactly* what they said about the coelacanth, so cryptozoologists tend to take what conventional science has to say with a very large pinch of sodium chloride.

The kongamato is a truly beautiful animal and there is much pleasure to be gained from watching as it soars high above, then swoops majestically down to the river to overturn a boat or two. They don't mean any actual *harm* by this, in much the same way that a cat playing with a mouse doesn't mean any actual harm. It's just a game.

You will find the kongamato is equally at home in its native Africa or any urban area you might choose. Of course, it may struggle to swoop majestically in between the skyscrapers but will nevertheless give it a damn good try…and will get just as much pleasure from flipping over a narrowboat on the local canal as a small canoe on a wide, raging African river.

You will want to ensure you have the right food for your pet. This can be purchased via mail order and it's as well to make sure you get your order in on time because if you run out you will find the kongamato is not the most obliging pet when it comes to making do with whatever is left in the fridge until the order is delivered.

Their diet mostly consists of a specially formulated dried kibble, but some kongamatos are thought to have developed a taste for decaying flesh, and are not too proud to dig up a body if they feel a bit peckish. Please bear this in mind if you live anywhere near a graveyard, as digging up Great-uncle Cornelius is considered very poor taste, and in any case it's probably a breach of local authority bylaws.

FAUN/SATYR

In Roman mythology fauns are woodland spirits, not unlike the Greek satyrs. Both these creatures are half-man, half-goat – the main difference being that fauns have hooves while satyrs generally have human feet. Usually these are size 12 human feet (or even larger) – this can make shoe shopping an absolute nightmare.

ROD

THIS ONE USED TO BE TERRIBLY POPULAR AMONG BOTH CRYPTOZOOLOGISTS AND UFO HUNTERS, BUT HAS BARELY EVEN BEEN MENTIONED IN RECENT YEARS, MUCH LESS INVESTIGATED.

For those of you who missed the wave of rod sightings back in the 1990s, let me bring you up to speed. These are tiny, translucent flying creatures whose existence is known *only* because they have been caught on film – and even then, they are only visible if the film is played back at slow speed. No one has actually managed to capture a physical specimen. Even if they had, they probably wouldn't know it as these things are so small and fast-moving. You could have one in your kitchen and you wouldn't know unless you happened to film it.

Once upon a time, recording things on film was pretty much the exclusive preserve of Hollywood. Then came advances in modern technology and the ordinary man in the street suddenly got his hands on things like camcorders and eventually smartphones, all of which made it relatively easy for just about anyone to capture their own rod (on film at least). Hence the buzz in the '90s.

So here's the current situation: we have concrete evidence of the existence of rods thanks to the modern preponderance of recording technology, yet many experts still refuse to accept it as real. As a result of this the rod remains unclassified. Some say it is a UFO, some say it is an insect, some say it is the protrusion into our dimension of some other form of life. Yet others maintain it is simply a camera glitch.

What we *do* know is that it moves too fast for the human eye to see, and is only revealed when film is played back at a slower speed. For this reason it is unlikely to be a good choice as a family pet. Children have a tendency to want to actually *see* their pets fetching a ball, and the rod is not known for the ticklishness of its tummy.

Nevertheless, the rod remains a fascinating creature and is most assuredly worthy of study. Perhaps what is *most* interesting about the rod is how rarely it turns up in documentaries these days. As has been noted, back in the 1990s, the rod enjoyed almost as much publicity as Bigfoot, with teams of earnest investigators scouring the wilderness in search of this animal.

Nowadays…nada…nothing…zilch.

It's almost as if someone were suppressing the information, which is, in itself, highly suspicious.

When asked if the government is involved in a cover-up, a spokesman had this to say:

'No.'

This reporter went undercover to investigate further. When pressed for an explanation of the lack of publicity and research now given to the subject of rods, an unnamed source replied, 'Where's the regular tea lady? Just give me my Earl Grey and get out of my office.'

Well, I never said I was *deep* undercover.

CADBOROSAURUS

THE CHOCOLATE-LOVING DINOSAUR·

This lake-dwelling serpent is a native of British Columbia, and indeed this remains the only place it can be found in the wild. It was first catalogued in the Cadboro Bay area, and this gave rise to the name, which was quickly shortened to the more familiar Caddy.

This is your basic sea serpent, growing up to 20ft for a mature adult. Perhaps its most notable feature is its rather spiky tail. It is wise to avoid stressing the animal in case it becomes agitated and starts thrashing around what is essentially nature's answer to the machete. You will want to ensure none of your friends get in the way of this. Of course, on the plus side, if it becomes *very* agitated, there will be no one left to dispute your story at the subsequent police inquiry.

Generally, the creature can be calmed with a few chunks of chocolate, but be careful not to overfeed. Sea serpents absolutely *hate* getting spots.

Although this animal is not really suited to life on land, back in the 1980s some idiot in plus fours thought the nickname Caddy suggested it would make a great golfing companion. He was last seen being dragged feet first into the water hazard on a well-known golf course in the English Lake District. Naturally the exact location must be kept secret as any publicity may prove detrimental to conservation efforts.

The answers to the rather more puzzling questions of how the animal was transported all the way from British Columbia to Windermere, and whether it went through appropriate quarantine procedures, have so far eluded the experts.

CRYPTIDS FOR THE GENERALLY BEFUDDLED

A RANDOM SELECTION FOR THE CRYPTID
OWNER WHO SIMPLY CAN'T DECIDE.

SETONTOT

As a general rule, hairy bipedal primates are not known for their sense of humour. This 7ft-tall animal from Malaysia is different.

When the boss makes a joke at work, everyone laughs, regardless of whether or not it was actually funny. Well, it's a bit like that with the setontot. Who is going to tell a 7ft-tall ape that it's a jerk?

The setontot's favourite game is to hide in the bushes and leap out at people shouting something blood-curdling that sounds a bit like, 'Rreeeeaaaaaarrrggghhhhh!' but which translates roughly as, 'Boo!!!!!'

This would probably not be so bad if the people on the receiving end actually *knew* they were taking part in the game. It can be quite unsettling if you're not aware of that fact, and you are struggling to find your front-door key while laden down with five bags of groceries, and *this* is the point at which the setontot chooses to pounce.

Yeah, that's a real barrel of laughs.

VAMPIRE

Everyone knows about vampires, right? At least everyone *thinks* they know about vampires. They know that one minute you've got a cute little bat chasing a ball of string round your living room, and the next minute you've got an incredibly sexy, irresistible and supremely elegant man in a tuxedo and cape who wants to bite your neck and suck your blood. And that all seems perfectly reasonable at the time.

One of the other things people know is how to *kill* vampires, which is a strange thing to read up on if you are thinking of homing a vampire, but I suppose it takes all sorts.

What people generally *don't* know about vampires, however, is that if you let the cat play with them when they are in bat form, they will remember this misdemeanour when they transform into human form, and will probably not be best pleased about it. It is really just asking for trouble to home a vampire if you have other pets.

Although they do prefer human company, they will not hesitate to abuse…er, that is, play with your other pets if the mood takes them. They can also be a jolly inconvenient sort of pet to have around if you have any vegetarian leanings. They require a very specialised sort of diet and generally their digestive systems cannot cope with soya milk and textured vegetable protein, which is a staple for many vegetarians.

Avoid any vampires who think it should be spelt 'vampyre'.

AGOGWE (SEE ALSO KAKUNDAKARI)

THIS IS ONE OF THE MANY, MANY APE-LIKE CREATURES SPOTTED AROUND THE WORLD AND DISMISSED BY SCIENTISTS AS BEARS OR SWAMP GAS OR THE PLANET VENUS (THESE BEING THE DEFAULT EXPLANATIONS FOR JUST ABOUT EVERYTHING).

The agogwe may be sourced in the forests of East Africa, though this may be a little too far for some people to go just to choose a pet. On the upside, however, the agogwe looks great in baggy shorts and a loud floral shirt and should sail through Customs no problem at all if you can teach it to say, 'Peace, man!' with a faraway look in its eyes.

The mature agogwe reaches approximately 4ft in height, and has long, somewhat unkempt, coarse woolly hair.

Agogwe vulgaris, the common rust-coloured variety, is available from a number of authorised breeders, and is really very easy to source. The black or grey agogwe (*Agogwe sophisticus* – an altogether more refined hairy bipedal primate, this one will delicately stick out his pinkie finger while tearing you limb from limb) is, however, far more highly prized and really quite rare.

These animals can only be found through an exclusive listing of authorised breeders, most of whom are fully aware of the rarity of the product and will therefore fleece you. Er…that is, they will charge you what they consider to be a fair rate…which, in basic terms, means they may just leave you with your bus fare home if they are feeling particularly warm and fuzzy. But don't count on it.

Once you have procured your agogwe, be it of the *vulgaris* or *sophisticus* variety, you will find it needs about as much care as the average human teenager, which is to say as long as you feed and water it regularly and don't expect it to actually hold a conversation with you, things should go swimmingly.

They are prone to problems if the fur is allowed to become straggly, so it is recommended that the coat is clipped at the start of summer. This is not something to tackle on your own unless you are very experienced and totally confident in your abilities. If you have a large family to help pin him down, this could be an unusual way to spend a dull Sunday afternoon. You should, however, be prepared to wake one morning soon after, to find approximately two-thirds of your scalp will have been shaved.

This is merely the agogwe's attempt at reciprocal grooming and should not be interpreted as a sign of aggression. Indeed, if you appear anything less than thrilled with the results you will quickly discover just how vulgar *Agogwe vulgaris* can be.

EATS	Just about anything. Particularly partial to chicken and mushroom-flavoured noodles.
LIKES	Hunting and gathering. Needlepoint. Having its tummy tickled. Getting caught in the rain.
DISLIKES	Loud shirts. People who change lanes without indicating.

KAKUNDAKARI

Here we consider whether the kakundakari and the agogwe are actually just different names for the same species, and ask if it even matters.

Once you have adopted your new pet, you will quickly learn to love it and mere nomenclature will mean little, unless of course you are the type who cares about the fine print in the Breeders' Association handbook.

Yes, OK, it has to be said, some of the top people in the Association are a little tetchy about this issue and may decline your registration, but such minor irritations count for little when you have the love and affection of your very own kakundakari…or agogwe.

XING XING

THE SECRET AGENT OF THE CRYPTOZOOLOGY WORLD, THIS MYSTERIOUS ANIMAL FROM THE HIMALAYAN MOUNTAINS IS A VERITABLE MASTER OF DISGUISE.

It has been described variously as:

Small.

10ft tall.

Orange/reddish in colour.

Black in colour.

A primate.

A Japanese sea serpent with a penchant for alcohol.

Who *wouldn't* want to own one of these? Think of the hours of fun you could have playing hide and seek with your pet, with the added thrill of never being entirely certain of *exactly* what it is you are seeking.

This is also a significant advantage when it comes to regulatory permissions because, let's face it, if they can't accurately describe the animal, they are going to have one hell of a job prosecuting you for not having a licence for it.

DROP BEAR

Related to the koala but scoring significantly lower on the cuddly scale, the drop bear is larger and more aggressive than its cousin, and decidedly more devious.

They are known to hide in trees and drop on the heads of their prey. This could provide a jolly wheeze for one of those company team-building exercises out in the woods, where people who day-to-day cannot abide one another will be persuaded to shoot little pellets of coloured paint at each other and pretend that they really didn't mean it to hurt. Honest.

CANVEY ISLAND MONSTER

THIS RARE MARINE ANIMAL PROVIDES US WITH AN EXCELLENT EXAMPLE OF OPENNESS AND TRANSPARENCY IN SCIENCE.

In November 1953 a mysterious corpse was washed up on the shore of Canvey Island, Essex, UK. After a brief examination by unnamed zoologists it was hastily cremated, and a brief statement was issued to the public declaring it to be nothing unusual, and certainly of no defence significance. Well, *almost* certainly.

What could possibly be more open and transparent than that?

Another carcass washed up onshore the following year, giving rise to concerns about the viability of the species in this region. The experts wrung their hands and looked worried quite a lot…and then stories began to emerge suggesting that it was nothing more unusual than an anglerfish.

Seriously? *That's* the best cover story they could come up with?

This second specimen was also studied 'officially' and amid much hand-wringing, the experts (unnamed, naturally) leapt hastily into action and failed completely to produce any official explanation of the classification of the carcass or what, in fact, had happened to it.

Reliable sources reported the animal to be 4ft in length and reddy-brown in colour. Although this description may bear some slight superficial resemblance to the anglerfish, well, that's like saying that just because Fred Bloggs from down the road has ginger hair, it's perfectly reasonable to infer that he's actually Chris Evans, who has merely adopted the 'Fred Bloggs From Down the Road' persona in order to go to the local chip shop without being followed by hordes of paparazzi. Some people are just so gullible. Honestly, if you want to get anywhere in this cryptozoology lark you really have to learn to read between the lines.

Although described as a fish (though definitely NOT an anglerfish…got that?), the creature is reported to have had legs. Rumours persist about the creature's legs actually being misidentified fins…which is clearly all part of the cover-up. Do they think we were born yesterday?

EATS	Well, not that much actually, since most experts describe it as being dead.
LIKES	Lazing on the beach.
DISLIKES	So-called 'experts' who come along and wring their hands, prod at it and then declare it to be of no defence significance…or an anglerfish.

DAHU

This poor animal has been tormented by French and Swiss mischief-makers for years. It's basically a common-or-garden mountain goat, but it does have one, rather interesting, distinction, in that it has evolved the peculiar trait of having legs longer on one side than the other. This enables it to walk easily around the side of steep mountains, although the obvious downside to this is that it can only walk *one way* around the mountain.

The authorities claim this is nothing more than a hoax (well, they *would* say that, wouldn't they?), and many gullible tourists have been persuaded to join in the dahu hunt, in which one person will climb the mountain and startle the dahu so that it loses its balance and tumbles to the bottom, where the other person is waiting to catch it.

Animal rightists are very much opposed to this barbaric blood sport, and there is a growing movement dedicated to the protection of the dahu.

Groups of peace-loving campaigners can be seen around the foot of the mountains every weekend, doing their level best to disrupt the hunts. Unfortunately this has been met with only limited success since most of the hunts are actually conducted on Tuesdays and Thursdays, when the peace-loving campaigners are at home watching daytime telly.

A number of celebrities have been approached in an attempt to get them to wear the iconic 'Save the Dahu' T-shirt and join in the protest marches. Sadly, none have yet responded, but given the vital nature of the protest work, this is surely just a matter of time.

ORANG PENDEK

THIS IS ONE OF THE MANY, MANY HAIRY BIPEDAL APES FOUND IN COUNTLESS PLACES AROUND THE PLANET.

There are so many sub-species that it's frankly amazing that science still refuses to recognise them as real. It's rather like denying the existence of lions simply because we already know about tigers, so that must be it for cats, right?

The orang pendek is a particularly short version, generally only reaching about 4ft in height. It isn't terribly bright, but it is friendly, and especially likes to have its tummy tickled. If you are the sort of person who likes miniature animals, this could be the ideal pet for you.

It has been suggested that the orang pendek is merely another one of those branches on the human family tree, where we diverged thousands of years ago and haven't spoken since.

The discovery of *Homo floresiensis* remains (better known as the 'hobbit') in Indonesia in 2003, has given some credibility to the theory that there really *could* be other primate species out there, as yet undocumented and unrecognised (and therefore *unregulated*) by science.

So, what this means for the aspiring cryptid owner is pretty clear. If you want one of these you really need to move fast. Once this thing is officially declared real, there will be no end to the paperwork involved in homing one.

INTULO

The Intulo is basically a bipedal primate, but don't get all mushy thinking this is another snuggly-cuddly-huggle-monster from the bigfoot genus. No, these guys are totally different – a little freaky and a little scary, to be blunt.

The intulo is a bipedal primate with a difference – reptilian features, and we're not just talking about snake eyes. These are lizard-like creatures with human characteristics, and probably not the nice characteristics that you'd want Uncle George to read out to the assembled throng when toasting you at your surprise birthday party.

The intulo lives in the South African province of KwaZulu Natal, but similar creatures have been reported right across the globe. They grow to around 6–7ft tall, and prefer to live in forested and swampy areas…mostly because such an environment affords them unrivalled privacy while they conduct their observations…of *us*.

An ancient, almost forgotten pathway weaves its way through the province, and there have long been reports of lone ramblers making their way boldly into the wilderness and demanding right of access, only to emerge days later, wild-eyed, and telling crazy stories of being captured by strange, unknown creatures and forced to undergo all kinds of bizarre tests. Some claim to have been subjected to nothing more invasive than a few seriously weird Rorschach tests, while others report days at a time spent wandering around a maze before eventually stumbling upon a reward of a cup of tea and a slab of Kendal Mint Cake.

Naturally these reports have all been dismissed as 'unconfirmed' or 'uncorroborated'. Indeed, sometimes phrases like 'complete and utter poppycock' have even been bandied about, and it has been suggested that nothing more exotic than toxins in the local plant life are to blame for these hallucinogenic odysseys.

Some suggest that the intulo are starting to branch out and conduct their research on a significantly grander scale. We can only guess at their motives in engineering the proliferation of crass reality television programmes, but the mind-numbing effect on modern civilisations is obvious –leaving human populations vulnerable to… well, to whatever it is that evil, power-crazed reptilians do.

It has been suggested that the intulo are illegal aliens, by which I don't mean they've left their passports on the kitchen table underneath a half-empty jar of marmalade…I mean they're from a different planet entirely, probably even a different galaxy.

Don't bother with this species as a pet. If they're bright enough to travel thousands of light years across space, with all the intellectual and technological requirements and capabilities that implies, then they're unlikely to be satisfied with a life competing in Best of Breed competitions and begging for table scraps.

On the other hand, if they've travelled thousands of light years across space, with all the intellectual and technological requirements and capabilities that implies, and yet they *still* choose to make their home in a swamp, then perhaps begging for table scraps would qualify as high entertainment and chasing their own tail is merely an intellectual aspiration.

EPILOGUE

If, having read this book, you still feel that you need a cryptid in your life (and let's face it, what home isn't going to be improved by the addition of an uncatalogued, unregulated and untamed drain on your food supply?), you will need a few essentials:

A kind heart.
A loving home.
A big cage and a bloody good supply of bandages.

Whatever pet you eventually choose, remember it will be with you for life, not just for Christmas (that is, unless it's one of those pets that is likely to eat you before the echoes of 'Jingle Bells' have faded).

Good luck in your ventures – you are now a member of the cryptozoology community, that happy band of intrepid adventurers putting the search for knowledge above personal safety, common sense and beige carpet.

DISCLAIMER

The author accepts no responsibility whatsoever for any ill health, injury, fatality or embarrassment (imagined or otherwise) arising from, or in any tenuous way related to, usage of this book.

If you can't take a joke you probably shouldn't be homing anything more exotic than a painted pebble.

In short, if you get bitten, scratched, eviscerated or otherwise inconvenienced, it's entirely your own fault, pal.

For Mum and Dad,
Mike, Peter and Amy

First published in the United Kingdom in 2016 by
Portico
1 Gower Street
London
WC1E 6HD

An imprint of Pavilion Books Company Ltd

ISBN 978-1-91104-226-6

A CIP catalogue record for this book is available from
the British Library.

10 9 8 7 6 5 4 3 2 1

Reproduction by Mission Productions Ltd, Hong Kong
Printed and bound by Toppan Leefung Printing Ltd,
China

This book can be ordered direct from the publisher at
www.pavilionbooks.com